E.J. RUSSELL

Mystic Man

Cover art: L.C. Chase, https://lcchase.com
Edited by Tricia Kristufek

ISBN: 978-1-965284-00-1

First edition
June 22, 2018

Contact information:
ejr@ejrussell.com

E.J. RUSSELL

MYSTIC MAN

For Jim, who—despite over thirty years in Oregon—is still a Connecticut Yankee at heart.

CHAPTER ONE

The ocean's on the wrong side.

The sun, tipping toward the west, wasn't aiming for the sea that lurked out of sight at the mouth of the Mystic River. That, more than anything—more than typing his scathing letter of resignation, more than his brief conversation with an openmouthed real estate agent, more than buying a last-minute, *full-price* ticket from LAX to Hartford—brought home to Aaron the enormity of what he'd done.

I'm on the other side of the country without a safety net—no friends, no home, no job.

Correction: no job *yet.* Fingers twitching, panic fizzing in his veins, Aaron fumbled his phone out of his pocket and pulled up his calendar app. Tomorrow the entire afternoon was blocked out in comforting green. *Interview and presentation at Hillview Academy.*

He'd applied for the job of librarian-slash-history teacher on an impulse anyway, his sinuses burning from over an hour in rush-hour traffic on a day with yet *another* air quality advisory, frustrated with the latest mind-numbing research assignment in the ad agency's poorly scanned, unindexed archives. When the school had scheduled his first phone interview, he'd assumed it was a fluke, so he hadn't been nervous. *That must have been why it went so well—I had nothing at stake then.* The second interview—same thing.

When he got the call for the third interview, he'd been on his lunch hour, just leaving the food court at the mall. He was about to agree to meet with a local alumni committee when he'd spotted his ex in the jewelry store, cooing over wedding rings with his new boyfriend not two months after Wayne had walked out, claiming he *wasn't the marrying kind.*

So Aaron blurted, "You needn't go to the trouble. I'm relocating to Connecticut anyway. Leaving tomorrow, in fact, so I'd be happy to visit the campus and meet with the committee there."

What the hell was I thinking? I'm never *spontaneous. I* always *plan and plan again.* Yet he'd let hurt and humiliation goad him into the first impulsive decision in his entire thirty-seven years, completely imploding his life.

He'd never even been out of Southern California before. Hell, in the sandwich shop where he'd stopped to buy lunch this afternoon, he'd stared at the chip rack for ten minutes, unable to find any recognizable brands. What made him think he could navigate an entirely new state where even the damn potato chips were strangers?

He blotted the perspiration off his upper lip. Maybe it wasn't too late for a reset. The HR manager at the agency had always been nice to Aaron. Maybe he could talk her into forgetting about that unfortunate resignation letter. Hillview had told Aaron he was one of three final candidates—they'd have no problem filling the post.

That's what he'd do. Cancel his interview. Text the real estate agent to take his condo off the market. Book yet another full-price ticket. Fly back to Southern California. With his boss away on his annual self-discovery retreat, chances were good that nobody but the HR manager would even know he'd been gone.

He cast a last wistful glance at the charming historic houses surrounding the Mystic Seaport Village green. He'd come this far. Maybe he could delay another few hours to tour the museum before returning to his hotel to pack.

No. He couldn't put it off. If this put a serious dent in his savings with nothing whatsoever to show for it, that should teach him a lesson that he'd apparently forgotten: *security is paramount.* "Familiar" might be unexciting, but at least it was safe.

His phone vibrated in his hand, and when he checked the screen, the text from the real estate agent sent his stomach into free fall.

Great news! Three offers on the condo in the first day. All over the asking price, and no contingencies. We'll be able to close even more quickly than you'd hoped.

No. No, no, no. This couldn't be happening. He'd set the price ridiculously high, even by Orange County standards, specifically to give himself a seller's remorse emergency escape option. But if there were no contingencies, and the offers were over the asking price, he couldn't pull out of the contract without a penalty—which his finances couldn't support. His savings still hadn't recovered from the condo down payment, and after further decimating them with two outrageously expensive airline tickets?

He dropped his arm to his side, fingers numb around his phone, alone in the crowd of laughing tourists. *Jesus, I'm as reckless and foolhardy as my parents.*

What am I going to do?

"Please, Uncle Cody. I want you to see my history report before I turn it in tomorrow."

Kaya's voice held that wheedling note that Cody could never resist. "I'll try, but—"

"Daddy's making tikka masala."

Cody laughed as he made his way down the path from the Seaport's Sailing Center. "Why didn't you say so in the first place?"

"Because," Cody's sister cut in, obviously retrieving her phone from Kaya, "you should want to come for something besides the food."

"It's not like I never see you, Eliza. I live in your attic, for crying out loud."

"Yes, you do, which is why it's amazing that you manage to go ghost on us as much as you do."

He rubbed the back of his neck. "About that...."

"Cody." Whereas some guys' big sisters' voices might rise to a shriek on a warning like that, Eliza's voice dropped to a growl. "Seriously? You're leaving *again*?"

"Um... yeah. I've got the money now to take that solo backpacking trip I was telling you about. As soon as I decide between Spain, Peru, or Bali, I'm ready to go."

"Alone? To a foreign country?"

"Lots of people do it, Lize, it's not that big a deal."

Her sigh was clearly audible over the phone. It was probably audible from Hartford. "How long this time?"

"I don't know. Four or five months, maybe? I want to be back in time for next year's spring tourist season at the Seaport. Don't worry. I'll keep paying the rent on my apartment, you hardass slumlord."

"I'm not worried about the *rent*, you doofus. We miss you when you're gone. And besides...." Eliza's voice broke, and Cody tightened his grip on the phone. His sister *never* got over-emotional unless....

"Are you.... God, Lize, are you *pregnant*?"

"Yes!" she wailed. "And you were gone on that stupid round-the-world sail when Kaya was born. You weren't there when I got home from the hospital. You missed her first smile, her first word, her first step. And now you're going to do the same with this baby."

Cody dodged out of the flow of visitors and sat down on a bench. "It's not for a whole year, Lize. How far along are you?"

"Three months."

"Then I should be home in plenty of time to welcome the new rug rat."

"What about Kaya? You know she adores you."

"She'll be tied up with first grade stuff. Even last year, when she was in kindergarten, she was so focused on her homework—and Jesus, homework in kindergarten?"

"It was just alphabet and counting practice."

"Well, Kaya treated it like the calculus AP exam. That girl knows how to focus. She won't even notice I'm gone."

"That's what you think. And if you don't show up tonight to see this project—"

"I should be able to. Don't worry. But why do I have to see it especially? Aren't you and Hiran supposed to award the official parental seal of approval?"

"She won't show it to us because you're the one who helped her with the research. She *will* miss you, Cody."

Cody sighed, his gaze traveling across the green to the dock where a steady stream of tourists marched up the gangway onto the deck of the *Charles W. Morgan.* "I'll miss her too. But I need to take this trip."

"Why exactly? You claim to love Connecticut. Volunteering at the Seaport. Even working for Hiran when he can nail your feet to the floor under your computer. Why do you need to keep leaving?"

Cody stood again and joined the people strolling around the green. "I don't know. Itchy feet, I guess."

"Free-spirited is one thing, Cody. Commitment-avoidant is something else."

"Hey. I'm committed. I volunteer here three days a week during the season. I'm at Mom and Dad's every Sunday. Downstairs with you guys probably more than you want to see me. But—"

"You're still looking for something."

Cody shaded his eyes with his hand and peered up at the sky. "Maybe." The angle of sunlight had slipped past that critical point—low enough to say "summer's over" even if autumn hadn't officially started yet. The change in seasons always filled Cody with an odd yearning that he'd never been able to identify.

He blamed Don Henley.

This time of year, post-Labor Day but before peak foliage season, "The Boys of Summer" always played on a loop on his internal playlist, with its melancholy reminiscence of times impossible to recapture, its vain search for someone no longer there.

Not that Cody had ever had someone to find—or lose, for that matter. But it made him *want*, as if his family, his beloved home, his *life*, was somehow missing a piece—although he had no idea what that piece might be. That's why he took off on some kind of adventure every winter.

"Cody, did you hear what I said?"

"Sorry, Lize. Say again?"

"I *said* I don't think you're looking for a thing or even a place—you're looking for a person."

"I've got Mom and Dad. You, Hiran, and Kaya. George, even though he's in Boston, but that's close enough for me." The last thing Cody needed was to have his perfect older brother around for comparison again. That had been enough of a pain growing up. *Oh, you're George Brown's brother. We expect great things of you.* He loved George—who wouldn't? The guy was perfect. But being constantly compared to him and found inferior got tiring after a while. "I don't need more *persons.*"

"You know that's not what I mean."

"Yes, but I'm giving you the benefit of the doubt, politely pretending that my big sister isn't trying to interfere in my love life. And if the reason you want me to come over tonight is to introduce me to another random guy—"

"No, it's not. I swear. It's Kaya's history report. She's so proud of it she's about to burst—goes around with it clutched to her chest as if we might try to sneak a peek."

Cody wandered along the path, enjoying the day and the ambience of the Village, one of his favorite places in the world, which was one of the reasons—other than his family—he always came back, no matter how far or how long he roamed.

"Fine. I'll be there, but you have to promise not to ride me again about signing on full-time with Hiran."

"But if you'd only—"

"I mean it, Lize. I love you. I love Hiran. I love his company. But I'm not ready to be an eight-to-five code monkey. Not yet."

"All right. But if—"

"Hold on." Cody tuned out his sister's continued squawks, because there was a *man* standing in front of the Cooperage—tall, lean, sandy haired, with the saddest blue eyes on the planet. He was looking around with a bewildered gaze, not as if he'd lost someone, but as if he was lost himself. "I've got to go, Lize. I'll see you tonight. Promise."

He hung up and tucked his phone away in his belt pouch as he approached the guy. *Oh wow.* He could never resist the bespectacled, professorial type, and this guy checked all Cody's boxes. He was obviously older— *another box: check!* But also obviously needed assistance.

And that's totally my specialty.

Cody glanced down at his outfit. He was wearing his Interpretation garb today—suede breeches, knee boots, linen shirt, and brocade waistcoat—so hopefully Mr. Sad Eyes would note the Mystic Seaport Volunteer badge and not think he was some random cosplay stalker.

"Hi." Cody donned his best smile. "You look like you could use some help. What can I do for you?"

CHAPTER
TWO

Aaron wrenched his attention from all the cues that screamed he wasn't in Kansas—or rather Southern California—anymore and focused on the man who'd just spoken.

The beautiful, smiling, *young* man. For a moment, Aaron was flattered that he'd attracted the attention of someone this appealing, but then he noted the period costume and the Mystic Seaport badge. *He's part of the experience. It's his* job *to help clueless, panic-stricken tourists.*

"I'm homeless," he blurted, then winced. "I'm sorry. That's not what I meant." He backed up a step. "I'll just be going now."

The young man held up his hands, palms out. "No worries. I guess if you've already seen all the Seaport has to offer—"

"I... uh...." Aaron had barely arrived before he'd taken that nosedive into panic, but there was a reason he'd come here. He was a historian, after all, and this museum was the most popular tourist attraction in Connecticut. "Not exactly."

"Oh. Are you waiting for the rest of your group?"

"I'm.... That is, I'm here alone."

"Really?" The man's smile was brighter than the sun on the water. "That's awesome. I think traveling alone is—well, I'm not sure, because I've never done it. I've always been with a few other guys. But the alone thing is totally on my to-do list for this winter. That's the way to meet people, right? To really get to know the culture?"

"I assumed that the reason for travel was to share experiences with the people you care about." Aaron gazed at the water that was definitely *not* the Pacific Ocean. "Alone, sometimes all you get is culture shock and never meet anyone anyway."

"Well, you're meeting me, right?"

Aaron's lips twitched. "You have a point." He glanced at his phone, sighed, and put it in his jacket pocket. "I suddenly realized that I'm completely at sea here."

"I guess you're not from around here." The man pointed toward the water. "Otherwise you'd know that to be at sea you'd have to sail down the river and out of the Sound."

"A smartass, eh?" Aaron raised an eyebrow. "Are all Connecticutters…. Connecticutians…. Hell, what do I call a Connecticut native?"

"Cody."

"A Cody?" Aaron's tentative smile faltered. "That doesn't track very well to 'Connecticut.'"

"It's my *name*, doofus." The man's—no *Cody's*—tone held a buried laugh.

"'Doofus'? I knew you had to be young. I didn't realize you were actually twelve."

"For your information, I'm twenty-six, but I have a six-year-old niece. I have to scale back my language around her, so it's easier not to backslide if I'm consistent all the time." Cody brushed his wavy hair away from his face. "Let's try this again, shall we?" He stuck out his hand. "Cody. Cody Brown."

Aaron shook the offered hand, keeping his face perfectly straight. "Aaron Doofus."

Cody's eyebrows shot up. "Seriously?"

"Of course not. Aaron Templeton."

"Wow. Now *that's* a serious name. You ought to be like a British MP or a reality star or a news anchor with a name like that."

"That's quite the range of possibilities, and not the obvious list for most people, especially those with young children."

"Why—Oh." Cody laughed, a bright, joyful noise that further soothed Aaron's jangled nerves. "Got it. *Charlotte's Web*. Don't worry. You don't look anything like a rat."

"Thank you. Your... er... colorful name is interesting. I thought *you* looked—"

"Twelve. Yeah, I get it."

"Yes, but besides that. Like Charlie White."

"The figure skater?"

"Yes. It's the hair."

Cody reached for his head, then stopped. "I... uh... need a haircut, I know. And it always gets blonder in the summer when I'm outside so much."

"Are you? Outside a lot in the summer?"

"Yeah. I'm a counselor at the Seaport's sailing day camps when they're running, and volunteer at least three days a week when they're not."

"Your employer must be quite lenient, then."

"Is that your sneaky way of asking whether I've got a *reeeaaal* job?" Cody grinned. "I work for my brother-in-law, but only on a contract basis. I'm a coder." He wrinkled his nose. "Yeah, Cody the Coder. Dorky, right? I swear I didn't choose computer science because of my name."

Somehow Cody had managed to get Aaron strolling along the path. "Actually, I think it's quite... evocative, in a *Sesame Street* kind of way."

"Oh very nice. And you accuse *me* of being a smartass?"

Aaron chuckled, the sound rusty in his own ears. How long had it been since he'd laughed? "Perhaps you're influencing me already."

Cody gestured for Aaron to take a right, past a small yellow house with a white picket fence. "So tell me. What was your favorite thing here at the Seaport? The planetarium? The Rosenfeld Collection? The *Morgan*?"

"Actually...." Heat infused Aaron's cheeks. "I've seen the ticket window and the green and you."

"And you were about to leave? Did someone force you to come here on a dare or something?" Cody's eyebrows drew together in a scowl that was out of place on such a sunny, open face. "You're not one of those dudes who hates history, are you?"

"Not at all. I'm a historian. I mean, my bachelor's degree is in history."

Cody's scowl vanished, replaced by an expression that Aaron would have called positively lustful if they were in a gay bar and not in the middle of a recreated nineteenth-century village. "You've got other degrees?"

"A master's in library science."

"Oh." By the disappointment in his tone, Cody's historian lust didn't extend to librarians. *Why does that disappoint me?* "Why not another history degree?"

"The MLS offered better job security."

"So." He clasped his hands behind his back as they made another right, circling the green with the river on their left. "Are you leaving in such a hurry because you've got somewhere else to go? A hot date, maybe?"

Aaron barked a laugh. *I have nowhere to go. Literally.* "Not today."

"But you're leaving before you give the Seaport a chance. That's not fair."

"I don't think the state's tourist industry will suffer because one librarian beats a hasty retreat." *With his tail between his legs.* "After all, I've already paid for my ticket."

"Maybe not, but in my opinion—" Cody shot Aaron a sly sidelong glance. "The librarian will suffer. Come on. What have you got to lose?"

Good question. It wasn't as if staying would be a hardship. A few hours in the company of a charming young man versus hours sitting in his hotel room or, if he couldn't talk himself off this particular ledge, at the airport. The distraction of the museum—and Cody's company—might keep his panic at bay.

The sun, the playful breeze, and the sudden bright laughter of a child racing across the green—not to mention Cody's eyes, the same blue as the river—made Aaron's decision simple.

"You've bagged yourself a librarian." Aaron held out his hand, which Cody shook enthusiastically. "And thank you." *More than you'll ever know.*

I'd like to bag myself a librarian. Fingers still tingling from the feel of Aaron's hand in his, Cody dialed back his NSFW daydreams. This wasn't a date, no matter how appealing he found Aaron. Although from the way Aaron had met his eyes, and didn't mind when their shoulders bumped or their hands brushed, Cody would bet anything he was at least bi if not gay.

Calm down and switch to tour-guide mode, you horndog.

Once he tore his gaze away from Aaron's square jaw and adorable wire-framed glasses, Cody spotted the perfect introductory exhibit directly in front of them.

"Right this way, sir."

"So formal."

"Don't get used to it. It'll probably be the last time."

Aaron fell into step beside him. Even though he was an inch or two taller than Cody, their strides matched. *We can walk easily together.*

Not a date, damn it, not a date.

Cody stopped in front the gray-shingled building housing the Mystic River Scale Model. "Here we are. Our first stop."

Aaron peered at the sign over the door. "A scale model? You're giving me a bird's-eye view first as an orientation?"

Cody grinned, pleased that Aaron got it. "Exactly. It's not the Seaport per se, but since you're a historian, you should appreciate it. This project has been going on since 1958. It's a representation of what the town looked like around 1870."

He held the door, so Aaron could enter. Inside the windows were curtained so that sunlight didn't interfere with the exhibit lighting. The two of them were the only ones in the building except for a family with a couple of preteen kids.

Cody led Aaron to the opposite side of the model. "This is one of the first things I worked on as a volunteer when I was about those kids' age. My dad and I used to work on models together—cars, spaceships, boats. He brought me here with him, and we worked on this together."

Aaron smiled at him, and Cody's stomach fluttered like a pennant. "You'll have to point out the parts you built."

"Nothing too major. I think I helped make a tree."

The family filed out, the kids making noises about ice cream. Cody stood back as Aaron circled the model, studying it with a concentration that brought an interesting combination of knitted eyebrows and a half smile to his face.

Cody walked in the other direction, part of his attention on the model and part of it on Aaron's reactions. *Yeah. He digs it too.* No matter how often Cody brought visitors to the exhibit, he never tired of looking at it himself, discovering the latest additions or noticing details he'd missed.

"What are you—" Aaron's voice jerked Cody out of his study of a new locomotive. "Are you actually humming 'My Little Town'?"

Oops. "Sorry." But when Aaron laughed instead of giving him a side-eye, Cody grinned. "What can I tell you? I was raised on my dad's music collection. My childhood had a soundtrack of music from before I was born. It left a mark."

"Is that so?"

"Yup." Cody joined Aaron next to the replica of the shipyard. "I admit to spending a *lot* of time looking at graffiti as a preteen, but I never experienced the least enlightenment."

"Let me guess—Simon & Garfunkel, right? 'The Sound of Silence.'"

"Got it in one. Apparently our local taggers aren't prophets after all, just people with poor spelling skills and no imagination. But I'm neglecting my official duties." He pointed to the center of the model. "A lot of the details are based on historical photographs of the town, and the ships were all known to have visited during the 1870s."

Aaron gestured to the covered windows. "Are the buildings in the Seaport full-sized reproductions of the same structures?"

"Oh no. All the buildings in the Village are historic trade shops and businesses even though they aren't necessarily from Mystic. The museum acquired them from other places in New England and restored them over time."

"I see. I didn't think any village could look this perfect outside of Disneyland."

Cody pretended to be outraged. "Hey. Nothing in Disneyland is older than the midfifties. These were all real houses, in actual use at one time."

Aaron held up his hands, palms out. "No offense meant. Although as a former Disneyland employee, I would argue that both Disneyland and Mystic Seaport Village achieve their stated missions. Those missions are simply different."

Cody blinked. "You know, I never thought of it that way. I've never been to a Disney park. I was always a little contemptuous of them for being purpose-built. But you've got a good point. Did you really work there?"

Aaron nodded. "When I turned eighteen, halfway through my senior year in high school. I flipped burgers at a restaurant in Frontierland. Not exactly the most glamorous of jobs, but it paid."

Cody chuckled. "I didn't have a paying job until I graduated from college. My parents aren't wealthy, but they're comfortable. They wanted me to learn to work for a different reason than a paycheck, which was why they started me volunteering so early."

Aaron's face closed down, and he uttered a noncommittal sound. *Uh-oh.* There was obviously a story there that made Aaron unhappy.

Changing the subject now. Cody pointed at the tree next to the general store. "That's my tree. I hope you appreciate its vast importance in the grand scheme of the model."

Aaron smiled briefly, but a hint of tension still lingered around his eyes. "Clearly a superior tree. What kind is it?"

"A green one."

Aaron laughed, and Cody felt unreasonably proud of himself. "If its progenitor has no clue, I don't feel bad for not recognizing it."

"Ready for the next stop?"

"I'm in your capable hands."

I wish. Cody led the way out of the building into the sunshine. "All the Village shops are fitted out with exhibits, but some have working craftspeople too. For instance"—he pointed at the Cooperage—"we have a cooper who builds barrels and buckets with period-appropriate hand tools."

"Very cool."

"Yeah, but there's someplace I want to show you next because it's got a great story behind it and you're a historian, so you must like *stories*, right?" Cody bumped Aaron's shoulder with his own, and Aaron laughed again

—but didn't dodge away. So as they walked past the Shipsmith Shop, their arms brushed with every other step.

Cody had to swallow twice, his mouth suddenly dry. "Here," he croaked. *Ugh. Way to sound cool.*

At least Aaron didn't seem to notice. Again, he studied the sign hanging outside the shop window rather than mounting the steps. *He's cautious—not one to dive into anything without consideration.*

"Nautical instruments?"

"Yup. After you."

They entered the shop, its interior full of mellow light from the bay window. Cody pointed at a display case. "Check it out."

"Wait—is this a chronometer?"

"You know the story?"

"Of course. The search for longitude. When the Royal Society offered their prize, they expected the resolution of the longitude dilemma to be elegant and spectacular, fabricated by someone—in other words, by a *man*—of a particular class and education. John Harrison, a self-educated clockmaker, didn't fit their upper-class expectations, and his invention"—Aaron pointed to the chronometer—"was simply well-engineered and practical. A craftsman's solution." He peered into the case. "Robert Kearns faced a similar bias."

"What did he do?"

Aaron glanced up at him with a smile that made Cody's breath catch. "He invented intermittent windshield wipers. Using parts from a blender, I believe."

Aaron straightened and gestured for Cody to precede him out of the shop.

As they descended the steps, Cody said, "I hope you don't think I'm overstepping, but I noticed you paused before you entered the shop. The scale model too. I'm guessing you're a guy who likes to look before you leap, even if it's just walking into a building."

"More like scrutinize before I leap—assuming I ever leap at all." He rubbed the back of his neck. "I'm afraid I'm not a very exciting person."

"But you made the trip across the country. By yourself?" Cody was fishing, he could admit it, but he wanted to know. "Or did you just shake off your family for the afternoon?"

That tension was back in Aaron's shoulders. "No family."

"Sorry. Don't mean to pry."

"It's okay." Although from the set of Aaron's shoulders and the edge to his voice, it was obviously as far from okay as it was possible to get. "It's something I have to get used to."

"Who told you that?"

"No one needed to tell me. When you have no options, you learn to live without them."

A kernel of anger burned in Cody's chest on Aaron's behalf. "You know what? Screw that. I say if you're out of options, change the rules and make some new ones."

"Ah. You're a rebel, then."

"Me? Not really. In school, my teachers accused me of daydreaming instead of attending to lessons. I'm a hands-on kind of guy, I guess. I like learning things that make sense. Stuff you can use." He jerked his thumb over his shoulder at the shop. "When I found out that geometry had a practical use in navigation, I aced it." He grinned.

"Practical navigation is a great lead-in to our next stop. Come on." He grabbed Aaron's hand and started to tow him down the path, but when he caught the astonished rise of Aaron's eyebrows, he let go. "Sorry. What can I say? Impulsive."

"Trust me. I didn't mind." Aaron smiled, and although it was small smile, barely a curve of his lips, there was a glint in his eyes behind his glasses that made Cody's heart dance a little jig.

He told it to pipe down. "There's a new exhibition hall near the north entrance that has some awesome installations, but I have to admit, I like my history in its natural habitat."

"You shock me."

Cody grinned. "Yeah, I know. Mr. Hands-on." Too damn bad he'd never get a "hands-on" session with Mr. Sexy Historian. But at least they had this afternoon, and Cody believed firmly in living for the moment. "And the Seaport is a great place for that."

"So you're a dyed-in-the-wool Mystic man, eh?"

"Hey. Dyed-in-the-organic-cotton if you don't mind. Wool makes me itch."

Cody led Aaron onto the wharf, the hull of the *Charles W. Morgan* rising before them. As usual, whenever Cody looked at the ship, his heart swelled with pride and awe. "Okay, Mr. Historian. Here's our crown jewel—the last wooden whaling ship on the planet."

Aaron gazed at the *Morgan*, his mouth slightly agape, his gaze following the lines of her rigging. "It's hard to believe people lived aboard boats like this for months at a time."

"Believe it." And since Aaron hadn't minded the touching, he tucked his hand under Aaron's elbow and led him toward the gangway. "And for the next half hour, you'll be living aboard too."

CHAPTER THREE

Aaron knew he shouldn't be intimidated by walking aboard the *Morgan*. He'd managed to board his first airplane to get to Connecticut, and the ship was about the same length. If he could spend six hours in a metal tube hurtling through the air, surely he could handle strolling around the open-air deck of a craft that was twice as wide and completely stationary.

So he ignored the dampness of his palms as he followed Cody up the gangway and onto the deck. "You know, I'm not sure whether I'm more appalled by the notion of living aboard a ship like this for years at a time, or by the activities it represents."

"Whaling, you mean?" The mast next to Cody was bigger around than he was. "I know. It's tough to think about. But we're looking at it from a modern perspective. The mindset back then was different." He nudged Aaron with his elbow. "You should know that better than anyone, Mr. Historian."

Aaron was grateful for the breeze cooling his heated face. "I know. But it's still hard to think about."

"I get it. You're empathetic."

Aaron shoved his hands into his jacket pockets. "Wonderful." In the days of Austen and Dickens, they'd probably have accused him of an excess of sensibility and called his panic attacks "vapors"—or else just clapped him into Bedlam.

"Hey." Cody gripped his shoulder and gave it a little shake. "Empathy is a *good* thing. Show me a guy with no empathy, and I'll show you a sociopathic jerkface."

Aaron couldn't help but chuckle. "Jerkface? Is that another niece-appropriate term?"

Cody's answering grin could have lit Aaron's condo— not that he still had one. "You guessed it."

"You'll have to give me the official translation sometime."

He nodded solemnly. "We can add Brownian to French, German, and Spanish in Google Translate." He patted the mast. "Check it out. The mainmast rises 110 feet above deck."

Aaron looked up, past the web of rigging, and a wave of dizziness swamped him. He grabbed Cody's arm as he swayed on his feet. "Whoa."

Cody covered Aaron's hand and squeezed. "Yeah, that's pretty much *everyone's* first reaction." He shaded his eyes and gazed upward too. "Can you imagine being the lookout? Up there, the deck would be tiny beneath you. Nothing but sky and ocean and an occasional seabird for company."

Aaron clenched his eyes shut, swallowing against a swell of nausea. "Don't."

"Shoot." Cody's other hand was suddenly warm on Aaron's back. "I'm sorry. Are you okay?"

Aaron nodded, swallowing twice before he opened his eyes. Cody's face was inches away, the breeze ruffling his hair and sending a few strands to tickle Aaron's cheek. *Close enough to kiss.*

Aaron dropped his gaze, the skin prickling on the back of his neck. "It's nothing. Just a momentary bout of mental acrophobia."

Cody chuckled, releasing Aaron to stroll toward the stern. "Not great with heights? My dad's the same. When we go apple picking every year, he makes sure to send me and my sister up the ladders."

"Sorry."

"No worries." His smile remained sunny as they wandered along the deck.

Aaron poked his head in the galley. "Holy crap. This thing is smaller than my closet."

"Not a lot of room for urban sprawl on board ship."

Aaron followed Cody below, down the steep, narrow stairs. Cody kept up a running commentary—tidbits about whalers in general and the *Morgan* in particular, including details about the restoration. His attitude was almost proprietary.

Cody patted the doorway between the mates' quarters and the blubber room. "This opening didn't exist on the ship when it was still a working whaler. The officers' quarters were physically separated from the working part of the ship."

"You know a lot about the ship. Did you help with the restoration?"

"As unskilled volunteer labor, yeah." He grinned at Aaron over his shoulder. "I scraped part of the hull. They let me paint a bit too." He stood aside to let a trio of other visitors exit from the room at the bow. "The ordinary seamen bunked in there, in the fo'c'sle. You've heard the term 'before the mast'? This is the place."

Aaron ducked through the doorway into the cramped area. The foremast descended through the middle of the room, bunks stacked two deep like a rat's maze around it.

Sweat broke out on Aaron's forehead. *So close to the water. Only a few inches of wood to separate them from breathing and drowning.*

His hands started to shake.

"I.... Can we go topside again? Please?"

"Sure." Cody was there immediately, leading Aaron to the stairs outside the forecastle and up onto the deck. "Is this okay, or do you need to go ashore?"

"Ashore, please. I'm sorry."

"Don't be." He kept his hand in the small of Aaron's back all the way down the gangway, leading him to a bench a safe distance from the ship. "The fo'c'sle is a little claustrophobia-inducing."

"It's not that. It's—Can you imagine trusting your life to something this small, this fragile? How could anything like this survive the fury of the ocean?"

"But it did. For eighty years. In fact, she was considered a lucky ship."

"Lucky?" Aaron's voice rose on the word.

"Sure. She survived storms, Arctic ice, hostile natives, a ton of trips around Cape Horn over thirty-seven voyages, and still made it back here so we could sail her again."

"But the risks.... Years-long voyages without the advantages of modern navigation or meteorological data." He clamped his hands between his knees. "And what if those sailors didn't come back? What were the survival chances of families, wives, children?"

Cody rubbed Aaron's back. "I'm sorry. I didn't know this would freak you out so much."

Aaron shook his head. "It's not your fault. Sometimes it just hits me, you know? The incredible fragility of life. All the people who perished in wars, from disease, in *childbirth* for God's sake. I'm constantly stunned that humanity has made it this far." He ran a hand through his hair, glancing sidelong at Cody. "Sorry. Like I told you, I'm not a very exciting person."

"You know, I don't think that's true. It's not that you're not exciting, it's that you've got two things that a lot of other people don't have." Cody held up two fingers. "A deep knowledge of the past, and an imagination."

Aaron choked on a half laugh. "You make those sound like desirable traits."

"Well, I think they are. I mean, who wants to talk to an ignorant person? And imagination? Heck yeah. If you've got an imagination, you can take trips, go on journeys, adventures, without ever leaving home, if that's what you want."

Home. Except he didn't have one now. But maybe…. He glanced at Cody again, who was gazing at the *Morgan*, a smile curving his generous mouth. Maybe finding a new home wouldn't be such a bad thing, not if it had people like Cody in it.

"You love that boat, don't you?"

He turned to Aaron, a glint of mischief in his eyes. "Don't let anyone hear you call it a 'boat.' It's a ship. There's a difference."

"Really? What?"

"You want the easy answer?" When Aaron nodded, Cody pointed to the whaleboat suspended above the *Morgan's* rails. "Size. A ship can carry a boat, but a boat can't carry a ship."

Aaron's breathing started to even out. He gestured to the side of the *Morgan*. "Where's the spot you scraped and painted?"

Cody studied the ship, his head tilted to one side. "It's on the port side, so you can't see it, but it's in line with the mizzenmast. My one square yard of the *Charles W. Morgan*." His face took on a dreamy, unfocused expression. "The day they launched her, after the restoration was complete, was the most amazing day. I'd have given anything to have sailed on the thirty-eighth voyage."

Chills chased down Aaron's spine. "You wanted to go on the ocean? In *that*?" The thought of such a precious cargo at the mercy of the elements nearly sent Aaron into tachycardia.

"Sure. It survived its whaling voyages with way less technology and support. And it didn't exactly cross the briny deep, you know. All the ports of call were along the eastern seaboard."

"That doesn't always mean anything. Margaret Fuller drowned less than a hundred yards from shore, lost along with her husband, her baby, and the only copy of her book on the Italian revolution."

A smile quivered on Cody's lips. "I'm not laughing at you, I promise. But did you specialize in the history of death and untold destruction? Surely there must be *some* cheerful history tales."

Aaron scrubbed his face with both hands. "God. There are. I even used to know some of them." With all the upheaval in his life, he'd apparently gone completely over to the dark side.

"Then tell me something good. Some historical event that makes you smile."

Of course, as soon as Cody said that, all Aaron could think of were *more* depressing stories. Richard the Third at Bosworth. Joan of Arc at the stake. The Spanish Inquisition. The Salem witch trials. The purposeful decimation of the indigenous North and South American populations by the invading Europeans.

Maybe happy people were too busy being happy to advertise their fates. Maybe humans were hardwired for drama, as if focusing on the misfortunes of others made your own life look better by comparison.

Or maybe we're just a race of ghouls.

"Having trouble coming up with something?"

"Sadly, yes. Give me a while to think about it, though, and I'll get back to you."

Cody grinned. "I'll hold you to that." He gazed at the *Morgan* again. "You know, the *Morgan* is a pretty sizable vessel, when it comes down to it. My round-the-world sail was on a ship more like that." He pointed to a passing boat no longer than Aaron's living room.

"You sailed around the world? On something *that small?*"

"Sure. It was awesome."

"How old were you?"

"Twenty. Twenty-one. I celebrated my twenty-first birthday at sea."

"Why on earth would you want to do that?" Just the thought of being adrift on the ocean, no sight of land, with who knew what kind of dangers lurking below—assuming the water didn't kill you first—made Aaron's belly attempt a reverse swan dive onto his shoes.

Cody gave Aaron that sly sideways glance again. "Blame it on Crosby, Stills & Nash."

"Crosby, Stills, and—oh. 'Southern Cross.'"

"Yep. I'm telling you, my whole life is like an oldies station."

"And mine is like the aftermath of every disaster movie ever made," Aaron said, his tone laced with disgust.

Cody laughed and stood up, offering Aaron his hand. "Come on. If you're not up for the shipboard tours, let's check out the planetarium."

"Indoors, surrounded by actual walls? I think I can probably handle that without breathing into a paper bag."

"Is it the presence of walls, or just the absence of ocean?"

"I'll let you know."

Cody held the planetarium door for Aaron to emerge, both of them blinking in the westering sun. "Yeah, the projector is from the sixties. Nowadays, a lot of planetariums use digital options, but the stars end up looking pixilated if they're not done right. But this one—"

"It was like we were away from light contamination, looking up at the stars in the middle of the night."

"Awesome, yeah?" Cody tucked his thumbs in the pockets of his waistcoat. "It was like that at sea sometimes. Crosby, Stills, and Nash got it right."

Aaron's shoulder brushed his as they strolled down the path. "Did that make the risk worth it?"

"I didn't really think of it as a risk. Maybe because I practically grew up on the water. Being out there... every day was a gift." He allowed himself to lean into Aaron's shoulder just a little. The path was crowded. Could be accidental, right? "Even when the other guys drove me crazy."

"So you weren't alone?"

"Nope. There were four of us. The boat belonged to a friend of my sister's. He needed another guy on the crew, and I jumped at the chance."

Aaron's expression turned pensive. "I don't know if I've ever jumped at a chance in my life."

"Scrutinizing before you leap."

He smiled crookedly. "Exactly."

Something about the sadness of that smile made Cody want to kiss it better. But although Cody had been accused all his life of being too impetuous, he knew better than to let his urges run away with him now. For one thing, this was the *Seaport*—practically his own personal church. For another, a guy as cautious as Aaron wouldn't appreciate it.

But Cody had seen the look of joy and wonder on Aaron's face by the light of the artificial planetarium stars, and he wanted to see it again. Wanted to *give* Aaron that again.

"I know you're not a fan of big wooden ships in general," Cody said, nudging Aaron to take a left past the Children's Museum, "but our Shipyard is working on restoring the *Mayflower II* now."

Aaron gave him some serious side-eye. "I think I can handle a boat—excuse me, a *ship*—that's not even in the water. I should have been able to handle the *Morgan*, but —"

"Hey. No judgments here. We can't board the *Mayflower II* anyway, but they've got viewing areas set up at the bow and stern, and it's pretty cool to see the shipwrights work. Plus, it might make you feel better about the *Morgan* if you can see just how *engineered* and sturdy these vessels are."

And as they watched the shipwrights hammering spikes with sledgehammers and shaving wooden beams with hand adzes, the tension seemed to drain out of Aaron's shoulders. When they left the viewing area, he wore the bemused, slightly preoccupied expression of a man whose mind was working overtime. *God, I love smart men.*

"That was... extraordinary." Aaron paused for a moment, shading his eyes against the setting sun as he scanned the Village shops, the river, the green. "This whole place is remarkable." He smiled at Cody then, with real enjoyment and gratitude, and a zing traveled straight down Cody's spine. "I can see why you're so devoted to it. What do you plan to wow me with next?"

Cody swallowed, his mouth suddenly dry, because *God, I really,* really *want to kiss him now.* If he had someone like Aaron around, someone to share these hometown adventures with, maybe he wouldn't be tempted to wander. *Because why search when I have what I've been looking for right here at home, surrounded by everything else I love?*

Cody opened his mouth, on the verge of asking for Aaron's phone number, but snapped his jaw shut. Because what was the point? Aaron was a visitor, a tourist. This was a one-day thing. He'd finish his vacation or business trip or whatever this was, then head home and straight out of Cody's life. Meanwhile, Cody would be off to—

He slapped his forehead. "Shoot! I almost forgot. I promised my sister that I'd be over for dinner tonight, so I really have to go now."

"Ah. Of course." The light dimmed in Aaron's eyes. "I've taken up too much of your time as it is. I appreciate you taking pity on me."

"There was no pity involved. If I'd let a newbie escape without at least one awe-inspiring experience, I'd have to turn in my volunteer badge."

"Awe-inspiring, eh?" Aaron grinned sheepishly. "Charitable of you to call it that and not what it was—a flat-out panic attack."

"Hey, everybody has their buttons. You should see my sister and snakes." He faked a shiver. "Brrr. Not pretty."

"Can't say I blame her. There's a reason I became a historian and not a herpetologist."

"Another phobia?"

"No. Just a judicious avoidance of animals who have their own agenda, possibly fatal venom, and a highly effective delivery system."

Cody laughed. "When you put it that way, it sounds perfectly logical."

Aaron raised both eyebrows this time, a double arch over the rim of his glasses. "That's because it is." He held out his hand. "Thank you again, Cody. This started out as one of the worst afternoons of my life, and you turned it into one of the best."

Cody was tempted—seriously tempted—to forgo the handshake and dive into a hug. *Or a kiss. Kissing would be really good. Aaron's lips were made for kissing.* But instead he settled for gripping that square hand, holding on maybe an instant longer than was technically proper. Then he waved as Aaron strolled away down the path, "The Boys of Summer" back on his internal playlist.

Damn it.

As Cody drove home and cleaned up for dinner, though, he couldn't get Aaron out of his mind. Oddly, instead of being off-putting, Aaron's innate caution somehow counterbalanced Cody's headlong rush at life. Aaron was open to discovery and new experiences—the look on his face at the Shipyard was proof of that.

He's just methodical. He needs to be introduced to new things slowly. Wouldn't it be great to introduce him to a new adventure and watch his expression morph from suspicious to intrigued to joyous?

And then to kiss him senseless until they embarked on a completely different kind of adventure.

Settle down, Cody Brown, his mother's standard warning repeated in his head. *Just because you thought he was hot, doesn't mean he felt the same about you.*

Not that it mattered. Aaron was just a tourist, and now he was gone. Cody rubbed his chest, trying to soothe the pinch of regret.

For him, I bet I could go slow. Real, real slow.

CHAPTER
FOUR

"Thank you for a fascinating presentation, Mr. Templeton. You kept our students engaged for the full hour." Dr. Kensington, the Hillview Head of School, smiled ruefully. "And I have to admit, that's not always an easy thing to do."

Aaron shook his offered hand, still a little buzzed from the tour and the presentation and everything he'd learned about the school. "It was my pleasure. The kids seem bright and enthusiastic."

"Enthusiasm," Dr. Kensington said dryly, "has never been a problem here."

"Well, they were delightful. I enjoyed everything about the day." Everyone had been welcoming, the interviews with the board, faculty, and student committees not as intimidating as Aaron had feared. And the campus, with its mellow brick buildings, towering maples, and meticulously maintained landscaping, was the kind of safe haven that Aaron had always craved. "Your school is remarkable."

"Thank you. We're quite proud of it." Dr. Kensington escorted Aaron to the parking lot behind the administration building. "You're our last candidate, so we'll be conferring shortly and making our decision. You may expect to hear from us within the week."

"I look forward to it."

Breathing in the crisp fall air, Aaron waited until Dr. Kensington disappeared into the building before stowing his briefcase in the back seat of his rental car and climbing behind the wheel.

This could work. It could really work. Because they'd liked him, he could tell. The two presentations—one for the faculty on his ideas for the library, and a lesson comparing actual Gilded Age technology to its representation in steampunk fiction for a lecture hall full of tenth-grade students—had gone as perfectly as he could have hoped. He might be risk-averse and borderline agoraphobic, but he knew and loved his subjects.

He flipped the keys in his hand, the rhythmic *chink* a counterpoint to his elevated pulse. Whenever he completed a big project, he always had this same reaction, this endorphin rush. Or was it dopamine? Whatever it was, it made him want to burst out of his everyday cocoon, escape from the habits he normally found so comforting, celebrate until the near-intoxication faded.

Wayne had gone along with it at first, but once he realized that Aaron's idea of celebration didn't involve hitting half a dozen clubs, getting sweaty on the dance floor with strangers, or tossing back enough shots to fuel a three-day hangover, he'd grown contemptuous and refused to participate.

But here in Connecticut, he didn't even have Wayne to douse his buzz with tight-lipped, barely concealed impatience. It dimmed his glee a little. Even if this did work out—and he had a really good feeling about it—he still didn't know anybody in the town, hell, anybody in the whole freaking *state.* It's not like he could invite Dr.

Kensington out for a chat and a couple of celebratory beers.

A grinning face haloed with blond hair swam into his mind. *I bet Cody would understand.*

Aaron sat back in his seat. Cody. A guy he'd met the day before and spent a few hours with. But when Aaron thought about it, even if he had another choice, he'd still pick Cody above anyone, even Wayne—*especially* Wayne —at this particular moment.

Because Cody understands the pleasure of little triumphs, of giving back.

Unfortunately, Aaron didn't have Cody's number. He'd been tempted to ask for it, but then Cody had announced his need to leave, and Aaron hadn't wanted to presume. After all, Cody was a volunteer at the Seaport. Shepherding clueless tourists around was his job. The time he'd spent with Aaron hadn't meant anything else to him, regardless of how momentous it had been for Aaron.

For a while, though, it felt like a real connection.

But that hardly mattered since Aaron had no way to contact him anyway. A little more of his postpresentation rush bled away. *I guess it's Netflix and pizza after all.*

Wait a minute—Cody said he volunteered at the Seaport three days a week. He might have another shift today. *Even if he does, who knows whether it's at the same time or if he'd want to see you again.*

"The hell with it," Aaron muttered, and started the car. If Cody wasn't there, he wasn't there. But if Aaron didn't look, he'd never know. "It's about time I learned to jump at a chance."

As he drove out of the Hillview campus and got back on the interstate to return to Mystic, he wasn't sure whether to congratulate himself for taking another risk, or curse himself for raising unreasonable hopes.

Cody waved goodbye to the family he'd escorted from the Sailing Center to the Children's Museum and peered at the sky. Another hour to go, if he judged the sun's position right. For some reason, his shift had seemed to creep past when usually the minutes sailed by like a ship before the wind.

He sighed. *Chalk it up to an Aaron hangover.* Even his sister had remarked at dinner last night that he'd seemed distracted. Kaya had noticed it too, refusing at the last minute to show him her report.

Oh well. He'd get over it eventually. Maybe not until the backpacking trip—which he'd never take if he didn't decide on his destination. He turned to head back to the Sailing Center and was suddenly face-to-face with—

"Aaron?" Cody blinked, his mouth falling open. It was as if he'd conjured Aaron with his mind, which was just nuts. Especially since in a gray tweed sport coat—with elbow patches!—white shirt, and blue tie, this flesh-and-blood Aaron looked even better than the imaginary version who'd kept Cody company since yesterday. And the smile lighting his face? *Ungh.* "What are you doing here?"

Aaron's smile faltered. "Oh. I.... You're busy. I shouldn't have bothered you." He shuffled back a few steps. "I'll just go—"

"No!" Cody lunged forward, startling Aaron into another backward step. "Sorry, I didn't mean to leap at you like some kind of psycho. I was just surprised to see you."

Aaron winced. "I don't have your number, but I should probably have left a message with the office or something."

"Hey. Just because I'm surprised doesn't mean it's a *bad* surprise. I *like* surprises." He offered what he hoped was a teasing grin. "Unlike some people."

Luckily, Aaron took it in the right spirit and chuckled, his earlier bright expression returning. "Yeah. That's me. Mr. Spontaneous."

"So, at the risk of making you bolt because you think I'm not glad to see you—which I totally am—what brings you back to the Seaport today?"

"Well...." Aaron rubbed the back of his neck, an adorable flush painting his cheeks. "You, actually."

"Me? You mean you shelled out the money for a ticket on the off-chance of running into me?"

"Well, I figured if I couldn't find you, I could go back aboard the *Morgan* and generate drama in someone else's life."

"You leaped."

He smiled. "I did. Straight at you."

A glow started in Cody's belly and headed north—and south. *Down, boy.* "Really? Awesome! But I thought by now you'd be on your way to wherever it is you're going next."

"That's the thing." Aaron's flush deepened. "I'm already there."

"Where? The Seaport?"

"No. I mean Connecticut. I just interviewed for a job as a history teacher-slash-librarian at Hillview Academy. I don't know for sure yet, but the interviews went great, and they liked my presentation, so—"

"Wait. You mean you're not just a tourist?" Cody's smile threatened to reach his ears. "You're moving here?"

"Yes. I mean that's the plan, assuming the job comes through and—"

Cody let out a whoop and grabbed Aaron around the waist, whirling him around in a circle in a crazy jig. "This is fantastic! We totally have to celebrate!"

Aaron laughed, although he stumbled a bit from Cody's unskillful, overenthusiastic dance lead. He stepped back, tugging his jacket straight. "I wasn't sure if you'd be interested in... you know... a low-key celebration with a guy you only met yesterday."

"Are you kidding? I've been kicking myself for not getting your number."

"Really? Me too."

For a few seconds, they beamed at each other like grade-school kids who'd just discovered a mutual love of Teenage Mutant Ninja Turtles.

Then Aaron blinked and shook his head like a dog shedding water. "My ex... well, he never got that I needed the release." His eyes widened, and a flush crept up his neck. "I mean, not *that* kind of release."

Cody patted his arm. "Don't worry. I get it." *An ex.* That was good. That meant Cody was free to crush on Aaron without worrying about being a home-wrecker.

"See, I've always had this thing, ever since I was a kid. Whenever I finished something major—like my seventh-grade science project, or a history term paper, or my MLS thesis—I get this rush, like I can't stay inside anymore. I need to get out and share it with someone." He shrugged.

"Not a lot of someones, which is what Wayne could never understand. Not a party. Just a… a…."

"A step outside the norm."

"Exactly."

"I know just what you mean."

"So you'd like to join me? Remember I'm not Mr. Excitement. I don't do bar hops and clubs and dancing until dawn."

Cody waved a hand in dismissal. "Pshaw. That's not the way to celebrate. All you get from that kind of celebration is a monster hangover and a boatload of regret—assuming you even remember anything about the evening. And how stupid is that? I mean, if you want to commemorate something, isn't the point to be able to remember it later?"

Aaron's eyebrows shot up. "That's… that's an excellent point."

"Besides, we're not only celebrating your new job—"

"Potential job." Aaron glanced over his shoulder as if he were afraid the Presumption Police might take him down.

"*Potential* job, then. We're celebrating a new Connecticut resident. If you're moving here, we need to start acclimating you. What do you say to a real New England dinner?"

Aaron's expression turned dubious. "Isn't that like boiled beef and rutabagas or something?"

Cody barked a laugh. "You're thinking of the classic New England *boiled* dinner, but that's not what I'm talking about." He dug his phone out of his belt pouch. "Do you have any food allergies?"

"Noooo." Aaron drew out the word, sounding more suspicious by the minute. *This is going to be fun.*

"Excellent. Let me make a call. Won't be a second." Cody always felt self-conscious when anyone watched him talk on the phone, so he half turned away from Aaron to speed-dial Eliza. "Hey, Lize. I need a favor."

He heard her sigh clearly, despite the shrieks from a couple of nearby toddlers. "What now? Don't tell me you're leaving town immediately?"

"No, you doofus. I want to take a friend out for dinner, and I need your organizational prowess."

"Hmmmm. I *might* be able to assist you. Is he hot?"

"Eliza!" Cody's face heated, and he turned even farther away from Aaron, who was mostly staring at his shoes, with occasional sidelong glances at Cody.

"Well, is he?"

Cody ran a hand through his hair. "You have no idea."

"Then I'm happy to help, especially if he's likely to keep you at home instead of gallivanting off to Tierra del Fuego or wherever. Wait...." Her tone turned suspicious. "He's not one of the people you're leaving town *with*, is he?"

"No. In fact, he's going to be teaching history at a prep school, so turn off your big-sister radar and pay attention. Here's what I need."

CHAPTER FIVE

Aaron was having second thoughts. *Yeah, like that's anything new.* An impulsive drive was one thing, but the way Cody was talking about this dinner date.... Was it a date? Cody tossed a glance over his shoulder, and the slight up-down look, coupled with the grin and the slight flush? *Oh yeah. This is a date.*

But was Aaron ready? He was still reeling from Wayne's betrayal. *Or was he?* He poked at that mental sore spot, the way he always did when he was tempted to go out and meet somebody new, and found that it wasn't the sharp pain it had been, paralyzing him, keeping him holed up in his condo night after night.

No, it was more like the residual itch of a days-old mosquito bite. Annoying, but not debilitating. *I can do this.*

But the way Cody kept talking about "the place in Guilford" rather than naming the restaurant made Aaron shift uneasily from foot to foot. Was the restaurant so out there that Cody couldn't even name it? Was he afraid Aaron would google it on his phone and refuse to go, the way he'd done when offered a second chance to tour the *Morgan.*

Aaron could hardly blame Cody if that was the case. After all, he had his phone in his hand, browser already pulled up on the screen, ready to do exactly that.

Not that he'd refuse to go wherever Cody suggested— he just liked to be ready for whatever awaited him. Being able to scan the menu before he arrived meant that there'd be no surprises. He could prepare himself for a particular dish. Wayne had always scoffed at him for that, just as he mocked Aaron for planning the meals he cooked and following his plans to the letter. But food was important. It wasn't something you should leave to chance.

His neck started to prickle, his palms dampening, a sign that his anxiety was about to spike. *Calm down. It's just dinner. Don't make a federal case out of it.*

Just then, Cody stuffed his phone into the pouch at his waist—and the historical costumes Cody had been wearing both times they'd met had nothing to do with how attractive Aaron found him. *Oh no. Not at all.*

He turned back to Aaron and stepped in close, just inside Aaron's personal space. "It's all set." He glanced down at himself. "I need to change."

"Don't do it on my account."

Cody's grin turned sly. "Like the outfit, do you, Mr. Historian?"

And just as had happened the previous day, Cody's playful attitude defused Aaron's anxiety. He allowed himself an answering smile. "You could say that."

"Good to know. But they're a bear to clean, and I'd rather not face a weekend of hand-washing if I trash this one tonight."

This place they were going had the potential to trash clothing? "Uh...."

"And you probably want to lose the tie and jacket. Not that they're not hot." He tapped the suede patches on Aaron's jacket sleeves. "Total sexy-professor look. But we're both off the clock now. You drove here, right?"

Sexy professor? Aaron fought the urge to tug at his collar, which was suddenly too tight. "Yes."

"Then how about this? We'll both go home and change. Then I'll pick you up at your hotel. Where are you staying?"

"At an Airbnb in Clinton." It wasn't particularly convenient to Hillview, but it had the best reviews in the state and was affordable—even given Aaron's current uncertain finances—especially since he could prepare his own meals. He gave Cody the address.

"Perfect. I'll be there at five. You're okay with an early dinner, aren't you? I figure you wouldn't want to let the postinterview euphoria dissipate before the actual celebration, but we could wait until later if you want."

Warmth infused Aaron's chest. How many people would think of that? However, it was exactly right. He'd have just enough time to shower and change, and the anticipation of spending the evening with Cody would extend his buzz long enough to get to the mysterious restaurant—where, with luck, Aaron wouldn't make a complete fool of himself.

"That's perfect. I'll wait for you out front."

Cody grinned again as he began walking backward down the path, away from Aaron. "That's what I like. A man who doesn't make me wait. See you soon."

Anticipation spurred Aaron to get ready so quickly he'd had to spend twenty minutes killing time on the Mystic Seaport website before heading downstairs from his quaint little rental only ten minutes before five.

Habitually early, Aaron had endured far too many instances of waiting for rides in the past from his mother, his father, Wayne—watching car after car pass by because they had either forgotten him (his parents) or simply had no sense of punctuality (Wayne).

He was ready to endure the same thing, but to his surprise, a battered blue Civic pulled up to the curb as Aaron reached the sidewalk. His heart leaped when Cody waved to him from the driver's seat.

Is he as eager to spend time with me as I am with him?

He opened the door and slid into the car. "You're early."

"I am." Cody leaned forward with an exaggerated double take between Aaron and sidewalk. "However, you were earlier—barely—so I don't feel like I should apologize."

"Nothing to apologize for. Early is good."

As Aaron fastened his seat belt, Cody studied him, his head cocked to one side. "You know," he said, a definite teasing edge to his tone, "you're already halfway to being a New Englander."

"What do you mean?"

"The khakis and royal blue polo. Very preppie. We just need to get a kelly green sweater for you to tie around your neck to complete the look. And naturally some top-siders with no socks."

"Top-siders?"

"A kind of loafer. The official footwear of the prep-about-town."

Aaron glanced down at his brown oxfords. "Isn't this okay?" Cody had on well-worn jeans and a blue T-shirt the color of his eyes. A navy UConn hoodie was draped over some kind of basket in the back seat. "I'm afraid I don't have any more casual clothes with me." Or at all. Another thing Wayne had always complained about— Aaron's lack of fashionable denim.

"It's perfect. Really, there are no rules where we're going. If you're comfortable in what you're wearing, I'm comfortable looking at you wearing it." Cody waggled his eyebrows with a mock leer.

Aaron was surprised into a laugh. "Well, that answers one question, I guess. I was wondering if this was a date. Is it? A date, I mean?"

"Do... do you want it to be?"

"I—Yes. Yes, I think I do."

Cody grinned, fanning himself with one hand. "Whew! I admit I was assuming, but you mentioned an ex so I figured you were more or less footloose and fancy free." He started the car and pulled into traffic.

"I don't think anyone has ever described me that way, but I'm currently unattached, yes."

"Great!" He glanced apologetically at Aaron. "I mean, not great that you're alone, not for you—unless you *like* begin alone—but great for me. Because I like you."

"I like you too. But there is something...."

Cody froze, staring straight ahead, his hands tight on the steering wheel. "What?"

"Where the hell are you taking me? Can you give me something more specific than 'the place in Guilford'?"

Cody blinked, his mouth agape, and then he laughed. He laughed for so long that Aaron was starting to get... well, not annoyed, but maybe a little uncomfortable.

"Sorry. Sorry. It's just—" Cody wheezed one last laugh. "Never mind. And now I absolutely will *not* tell you any more about our destination. We'll let it be a surprise."

"You know by now that I'm not a big fan of surprises."

"I'm betting you won't mind this one. So tell me, were you a teacher in California too?"

"Now there's a one-eighty in conversational subjects."

"Hey, we're in a car with a broken radio. And besides, I think it's rude to blast tunes at somebody rather than try to talk to them. You've got a history degree and a library science degree, and you're melding those together here, for the benefit of some of New England's most entitled teenagers. Did you do the same at home?"

Home. He still didn't want to think about that. "No. Actually, I worked in an advertising agency. I was in charge of researching copyrights, trademarks, and patents for new branding initiatives."

"That sounds... uh...."

"Boring?"

Cody grinned. "Well, I didn't want to *say* that, but since you brought it up. It just doesn't seem like something you'd like doing. I mean, it's pretty dry research, isn't it? And at the Seaport, you seemed more like a guy who's interested in history for the *stories.*"

Aaron stared at him. "You know, you may be the only person—including me—who's ever really gotten that."

Cody chuckled. "Maybe you should start hanging out with different people, because it seems pretty obvious to me."

Unable to come up with a reasonable response, Aaron looked out the window as Cody hummed "On the Road Again."

Their route didn't take them back on the freeway—or rather the turnpike. *For God's sake, even the roads have different nomenclature here.* According to the road signs, they were on Route 1, the Boston Post Road, and although they passed the occasional gas station or car lot or fast food place, it was still remarkably... rural. In Orange

County these days, you could hardly tell where one city ended and another began. The houses here were different too—shingled or lap-sided or brick rather than the stucco Aaron was used to.

"Aaaaand, here we are," Cody announced.

Aaron peered out the windshield. "You're taking me to Walmart for dinner?"

"No, doofus." Instead of turning left into the Walmart lot, Cody hung a right and then a sharp left in front of a little red house. There was a red and white sign in the grassy verge directly opposite its white door.

"Oh my God," Aaron blurted through his laughter. "The place is actually called *The Place*."

Cody circled the building and parked in a rough lot behind it. "I didn't mean to deceive you, but it never occurred to me that you didn't realize that was the restaurant's name, and then I couldn't resist."

"I think under the circumstances I might have done the same." Aaron climbed out of the car, grateful he'd brought a jacket since the seating was outdoors and the air was noticeably cooler with the approaching sunset.

"There. You see? You forgive me, and you're totally not freaked out by the surprise. Win-win." Cody opened the back door, tossed his UConn sweatshirt over his shoulder, and lifted out a wicker picnic basket.

Aaron eyed it, glancing between the giant basket and the restaurant. "So did we just drive here so we could look at it before we have a picnic on the side of the road?"

"Nope. This place is totally awesome. It's a seafood joint—lobster, clams, shrimp, mussels, corn on the cob. Some great desserts. But they don't have a lot of sides and they don't have a liquor license. So patrons are free to bring the extras with them." He hefted the basket and patted its bottom. "Wine, bread, and salad courtesy of my sister, Eliza. That's why I called her."

"I've... uh... never eaten lobster before. Not a whole one anyway."

"Really?" Cody's grin turned wicked. "Then I'm totally ready to pop your lobster cherry. Let's go."

Watching Aaron eat lobster was better than porn. The look on his face when he tasted the first succulent bite. *Oh my God.* Cody had to wriggle on his tree-stump seat to adjust his pants. And when Aaron sucked the meat out of the claws? *Just kill me now.*

"Mmmm. Wow. Man." Aaron licked butter off his fingers. *Gah!* "How did I get to be thirty-seven years old without ever having a whole lobster before?"

"I take it you're a fan?"

He grinned, his lips glistening with residual butter. "Are you kidding? I'm the new president of the fan club. Although...." He glanced at Cody through his lashes, a *totally* flirtatious look. "The experience is definitely enhanced by the company. And the ambience." With a lobster claw in his hand, he gestured to other patrons crowding the sea of red tables around them, the fire pit, their picnic basket. "This place—*The* Place—is great. Thank you. I can pretty much guarantee I'd have never found it on my own."

"Well, it's a much better experience with other people anyway."

To distract himself from Aaron's enthusiastic slurping of lobster legs, Cody topped off their wine. "So this is your first time in the state, and *obviously* Connecticut is now at the top of your list of favorite places. Out of everywhere else you've traveled, though, what's number two?"

Aaron ducked his head, fiddling with his corn cob. "I don't travel."

"Well, I mean, sure. I get that you're not a guy who sails the ocean blue, but on land anyway."

"Seriously. I don't travel. This is the first time I've been out of Southern California." He wiped his fingers on a wad of napkins and took a gulp of his wine. "I was raised in Fullerton, and I've never been farther south than San Clemente or farther north than Ventura."

Cody's jaw dropped. "What? Never?"

Aaron shrugged. "I almost went to San Francisco with my high school debate team, for the state speech tournament, but I didn't qualify."

"On purpose?"

This time it was Aaron's turn to goggle. "How would you know that?"

"Oh, just a lucky guess." Cody leaned his elbows on the table. "So if you're the kind of guy who hates surprises—and trust me, I've gotten that memo—why suddenly decide to change careers *and* coasts?"

"Well, it's complicated."

"Try me."

"Kangaroos and jewelry stores. With a side order of traffic and smog."

Cody blinked, his corn halfway to his mouth. "Huh?"

"It was a kind of evil harmonic convergence. We had a client who wanted to brand his company with a kangaroo logo, so my boss instructed me to find *all* instances of kangaroo logos within the current trademark and copyright window." Aaron took another healthy swig of wine. "Do you know how many companies use kangaroos in their advertising in the United States alone? And don't get me started on Australia."

"I can imagine."

"No, I'm pretty sure you can't. God knows I didn't. And most of the earlier instances haven't been digitized. It was microfiche and worse. The most mind-numbing thing ever."

Cody tried to imagine Aaron, with the bright intelligence and joy in his face at the Seaport Shipyard, stuck in a cubicle somewhere hunched over a microfiche and shuddered. "Nightmare."

"Absolutely. Then, I got stuck in traffic again on my way to work—which is, mind you, five miles from my... my condo—for an hour and twenty minutes. There was a smog advisory for the fifth day in a row. I was not happy —hell, I was barely breathing. Then, I hit the mall on my lunch hour—"

"The mall? You? You don't seem like a mall kind of guy." Cody grinned as he dug lobster meat out of the shell. "More a Lands' End catalog, 'give me one of each color polo and another dozen pairs of chinos' dude."

Aaron blushed, brushing at his plastic lobster bib with his long, tapered fingers. "That was a lucky guess."

"Nope. I'm just a very astute observer."

"Anyway, it was for lunch, not shopping." He sighed. "Bad move."

"What, the mall was infested with zombies and you had to shoot your way out?"

"Worse. It was infested with my ex and his new boyfriend. Of two freaking months, mind you. They were...." Aaron's gaze shifted to a point beyond Cody's shoulder. "They were in the jewelry store. Trying on wedding rings."

"Oh, man." Anger surged through Cody's chest, that some douchebag could do that to Aaron. "Was it a rough breakup?"

"In hindsight, it was probably for the best. But at the time, I thought a permanent hole had been punched in my heart." He met Cody's gaze again, his eyes so sad that Cody wanted to jump up off his tree stump and hug him. "The reason he broke up with me was because I wanted to get married and he... didn't. I guess he just wasn't interested in getting married to *me*."

"Jeez, Aaron." Cody reached across the table with both hands to grab Aaron's fingers, butter, lobster juice, and all. "I'm so sorry that happened to you."

He squeezed Cody's hands and then let go to pick a piece of Hiran's naan out of the picnic basket. "It wasn't your fault." He took a tiny bite of the bread, then shredded most of the rest of it over his half-eaten corn. "Besides, if he hadn't done that, I wouldn't be here now, right?"

"So what—you just decided to get the hell out of Dodge so you wouldn't see them again? You could always just change your lunch destinations, right?"

"It wasn't about avoiding them. It was about the whole —" He made a circle in the air with the remains of the naan. "—shape of my life. The job, the Southern California bullshit, the relationship that wasn't. I needed to change."

"You mentioned you were homeless the day we met."

"Yeah. Like an idiot, I put my condo on the market too. I found out I had multiple offers about a minute before you walked up."

"But an offer isn't a sale. You're not *actually* homeless, right?"

"No. But if I reject all of the offers—which are all above the asking price with no contingencies—I'll have to pay a huge penalty. And considering I quit my job before I got on a very expensive plane, my resources are dwindling."

"I get why you wanted to change jobs, and even why you might want to jettison the whole California rat race." Cody couldn't have stood it for a minute. "But there are a lot of places in the country who hire both history teachers and librarians, probably a bunch that do both, like Hillview. Did you look at other places? You probably had a lot of other choices."

Aaron picked up his wineglass with a wry smile. "To be honest, I only looked at Connecticut."

"Really? Why?" Cody offered to top off Aaron's wine again, but he shook his head. "I mean, Connecticut is awesome, but you didn't know that then."

"*Holiday Inn.*"

Cody paused, raising his eyebrows at Aaron. "Why would a hotel chain make a difference? You're not even staying at one."

Aaron chuckled. "Not the hotel chain. The movie. Fred Astaire and Bing Crosby. One of the local TV stations used to broadcast it every Christmas Eve, with the most egregiously offensive bits cut out, and my aunt and I always watched it together. It was a safe haven for me. Comforting. Something I could count on. Watching Bing

Crosby build his own belonging place despite everyone else's expectations."

"Okay. I'll bite. I take it Bing's belonging place is in Connecticut."

Aaron nodded. "There's a scene, after Fred Astaire's fiancée runs off with a Texas millionaire. Fred isn't even *in* the scene. It's between his manager and a guy who's, I don't know, a maître d'? A waiter? I was never sure. But when the manager asks if he's seen Fred, the waiter guy says yes. Twice—once when he asked for scotch and soda —a bottle of each. And the next time when he asked which way is 'Connect-i-cut.' When I saw my ex shopping for rings with his new boyfriend after telling me he didn't believe in marriage—the first thing that popped into my head was, 'Which way is Connect-i-cut?' I found the job listing online the same day."

"Well...." Cody's eyes prickled, and he gulped half his water to ease the thickening in his throat. "I'm glad you navigated your way to us."

Aaron smiled, gesturing to the remains of their meal. "I have to say, though, that my first experience is a lot less traumatic than Bing's first. I believe he fell into a snowbank."

Cody finished his wine, mind racing. If Aaron hadn't actually sold his house yet, he could still change his mind. *I need to sell him on Connecticut. I need to sell him on me.*

They topped off their dinner by sharing a piece of The Place's Mississippi mud cake, then packed up the picnic basket. Night had fallen by the time they walked back to the car.

"So how was losing your lobster virginity?"

Aaron's smile glinted in parking lot lights. "The earth moved."

Cody laughed. "Excellent. Well, since it went so well, how do you feel about another voyage of discovery tomorrow?"

Aaron's smile faltered. "Uh... voyage? I don't think—"

"Hey, it's just a figure of speech. No actual watercraft involved. Oh right." Cody slapped his forehead. "You're a *history* teacher, not language arts."

"You have to admit that my context with you has been very maritime-focused. I think I can be forgiven jumping to that particular conclusion."

"There, see? You can't leap into new situations, but you can leap to conclusions." Cody clucked his tongue. "Really, Aaron."

"I know. It's all part of that risk-averse thing. Expect the worst and you won't be disappointed."

"Well, forget that. What I *meant* was how about another outing—"

"Another date?" Was that a hopeful note in Aaron's voice?

"Yes. Another date. I consider it my sacred duty to introduce you to everything about my home state that will absolutely convince you that your first big risk was a success and you leaped in the right direction. Consider it positive reinforcement."

"'Positive reinforcement'? I thought you were a computer science major."

"I had to take other classes too. Psychology 101. It fulfilled my social science requirement. I know just enough to be dangerous."

He unlocked the car and stowed the basket in the rear seat. As he settled behind the wheel, he said, "I'm not just a tour guide at the Seaport, you know. I'm fully qualified to introduce you to the finest Connecticut has to offer."

"Is that so? What are these famous qualifications? Special training? An endorsement from the governor?"

"My birth certificate. I was born here." He pulled out into traffic. "Connecticut has everything you could want within a very short distance. You've got the ocean. You've got mountains."

"California has that too."

"Yeah, but in Connecticut you can get from one to the other in less than an hour. Hell, you can take a drive and hit all six New England states in less than six hours. We have *manageable*-sized states here."

"Manageable, huh? Well, it's true that Connecticut is barely bigger than LA County."

"Do you like hiking? That's safely land-based, right?"

"I'll have you know that I'm an experienced pedestrian. But how rough is the terrain? I've got running shoes with me, but not hiking boots."

Cody shot Aaron a grin. "Don't worry. The hills above New Haven are *manageable*-sized hills. No pitons or belaying pins required."

"Well, in that case, sign me up."

Cody pulled up in front of Aaron's Airbnb. How had he gotten here so fast? He should have detoured, maybe taken a drive along the shore, but no help for it now.

"Pass me your phone. Let's not repeat yesterday's mistake." When Aaron handed it over, Cody entered his contact details. "Can you meet me at my place tomorrow? It's closer to where we're heading."

Aaron accepted his phone and sent Cody a text, a wry smile on his face. "I am capable of navigating the roads, even without a sextant and a chronometer. Google Maps is a wonderful thing."

"About ten o'clock? We can have lunch on the trail."

Okay, now comes the awkward part. They looked at each other in the dim glow of the street lights. Aaron's glance flicked to Cody's lips. *Yes, please.* Given Aaron's look-before-you-leap nature, Cody didn't want to make the first move. He held still, tried for an inviting smile.

But Aaron opened the door. "Thank you. I had a really wonderful time."

"So did I. See you tomorrow?"

Aaron nodded and got out. He raised a hand in farewell after he closed the door, but didn't walk up the path. Instead, he stood, hands in his jacket pockets, until Cody finally convinced himself to put the car in gear and drive away.

CHAPTER SIX

The next day, Aaron was still kicking himself for not going in for the kiss. It was clear that Cody would have accepted it. *But is "accepted" the kind of kiss I want?* Wayne had sometimes acted as if Aaron's desire for closeness, for affection, was an imposition that he had to put up with in exchange for fucking.

Why did I ever think marrying him would be a good idea? Clearly Wayne had done him a favor by dumping him. *I should send him a thank-you note.*

As he was preparing to leave for Cody's, he checked his email, his belly dropping when his inbox contained nothing but the regular payment reminder from his mortgage company. *It's Saturday, for crying out loud, and my interview didn't conclude until after three o'clock on Friday.* He couldn't reasonably expect a response from Hillview yet. But then, "reasonable" had gone out the window the minute Aaron decided to take a running leap at a new life in Connecticut.

Dr. Kensington had said they'd notify Aaron by the end of the week. Hadn't he? Or was it "within the week"? Which week was he talking about? God, Aaron had been so high on the postpresentation rush, he couldn't remember much of anything.

I remember Cody's laugh. Cody's eyes. Cody's mouth.

Urgh. Not helping. He had a voicemail from his real estate agent—two in fact, both of which had arrived during his dinner with Cody last night. He'd been avoiding them, because she no doubt wanted him to make a decision. He wasn't ready for that.

He checked his hair in the mirror one last time—*what good will that do? It's not as if it ever looks any different*—and headed to his rental car, way too early as usual.

According to his phone's GPS, Cody's house was only ten minutes away by the turnpike. If Aaron showed up on the doorstep way before time, Cody would be forced to let him in, acting like he wasn't inconvenienced. Aaron had endured far too much of that with Wayne—although Wayne had never bothered to hide his annoyance.

Cody isn't Wayne. With his joy, his exuberance, the way he flung himself at life, he'd never betray his irritation—hell, he probably wouldn't even feel it. If his plans were overset, he'd accept the new situation and make it just as joyful, just as exciting, just as fulfilling as what he'd originally planned. *Spontaneous delight.* Aaron wished he could tap some of that himself.

But maybe I can bask in his, at least for a little while. And in the meantime, I won't strain it by being too freaking early.

So Aaron took an alternate route, the same one they'd taken the night before, with a couple of detours to explore side roads and drive along the shore. He managed to combat his chronic early-itis and pull up in front of Cody's house at nine fifty-eight.

Aaron had never studied architectural history, so he couldn't place the style of the three-story house. Maybe Victorian? But not the turreted, gingerbread kind. Whatever it was, with its cheerful yellow paint and white trim, it was charming and perfectly maintained.

Aaron mounted the wide porch steps, heading for the door on the far left that Cody had told him led to his apartment, but before he could ring the bell, Cody popped his head out of the other door.

"Hey, you made it."

Aaron lowered his hand and stepped back, checking the brass number plate over the transom. "I'm sorry. I thought this was your apartment."

"Oh it is. I rent from my sister and brother-in-law, remember?" He jerked his thumb over his shoulder. "This is their place, and since my niece is having a rough morning, I was hanging out to give her a little support. Come on in. You can meet some of my family."

"Uh... sure."

Cody held the door for him, and Aaron brushed past into a vestibule, a low bench on one wall and a line of coat hooks on the other.

Cody placed his hand in the small of Aaron's back and guided him into a sunny—empty—living room. "Keep going. We're in the family room at the back."

Ignoring the way his skin buzzed under Cody's touch, Aaron asked, "What's up with your niece?"

Cody slowed down, glancing through an arch into a short hallway before turning to Aaron. "She's upset because her teacher didn't like her history report."

"A history report? I got the impression she was pretty young."

"She's six." He smiled wryly. "Going on thirty."

"Six? What kind of report do they expect? I don't have a lot of experience with six-year-olds, but I'm pretty sure expository writing isn't in their standard skill set."

"It's an illustrated report. The kids pick some historical person they're interested in. Then the parents or, you know, extended family"—he pointed to himself with both index fingers—"help them research. The kids produce the artwork and present it to the class as a kind of show-and-tell."

"Sounds reasonable. Surely the teacher didn't criticize her artwork."

"No. But Kaya...." Cody sighed. "Let's say she tampered with the text."

Cody led the way through the hallway into a room with french doors that opened onto a deep lawn. The mellow oak floor and the deep orange walls, warmed further by the sunlight spilling in through a pair of bay windows, reminded Aaron strongly of pumpkin pie. He sniffed experimentally, expecting scents of cinnamon and nutmeg, but instead, the aromas were much stronger. Maybe... curry?

A man and a little girl were sitting on a brown corduroy sofa in front of a fieldstone fireplace, the girl's feet barely clearing the deep cushions. She had the same brown skin, black hair, and liquid dark eyes as the man next to her, so Aaron made the leap that this must be Cody's niece and brother-in-law. The man looked rather harried, and the little girl... drooped. She held a booklet, covered in green construction paper and bound with brass brads.

"Hey, Hiran. Kaya. This is Aaron Templeton, the guy I was telling you about. Aaron, my brother-in-law, Hiran Chaudhri, and my niece, Kaya Chaudhri-Brown."

Hiran stood up and shook Aaron's offered hand. "Pleased to meet you."

"My pleasure entirely."

"Aaron's a historian."

Kaya looked up from under her bangs. "I *hate* history."

"Kaya!" Hiran's tone was admonitory but tempered with an obvious kindness.

"It's okay." Aaron smiled down at the girl, who was wearing a Dinosaur State Park T-shirt that matched her pink high-tops. "It's not everyone's cup of tea."

Cody dropped down on the sofa next to Kaya. "But you were so excited about it. I seem to remember reading about three hundred and seven internet pages about Amelia Earhart with you last week."

"That was *before*," Kaya said darkly.

Hiran's pocket beeped, and he pulled out his cell phone. He winced at the screen, then glanced at his daughter, obviously torn between the message and the distressed little girl, who was glaring at her feet, kicking her high-tops together.

The phone rang, and Hiran clutched his hair. "I'm sorry. The entire team is about to melt down. I must—"

Cody shooed him toward the door. "No worries, BIL. We've got this." He gestured to the sofa on the other side of his niece, and Aaron sat down gingerly as Hiran strode out of the room. "What changed your mind, munchkin?"

"I'm not a munchkin, Uncle Cody. They wear stupid shoes." She punctuated her words with a double kick of the pink high-tops.

"Sorry, munchkin."

"Uncle *Cody!*"

Aaron wondered what Cody was up to until he noticed that Kaya's sadness had morphed into indignation. *Ah. Redirection.* Apparently Cody wasn't afraid to take one for the team.

Cody leaned into the cushions and dropped an arm across the sofa back, behind Kaya. His fingers brushed Aaron's shoulder, prompting an involuntary shiver.

He tapped the little booklet in Kaya's lap. "Why don't you tell us what the problem is? You wouldn't let me see the final project at dinner the other night."

"That's because it wasn't *done*."

"Well, it's done now. Can we see it?"

She clutched the booklet to her chest. "No. Ms. Jenkins said it was *wrong*."

Aaron didn't miss the flash of anger in Cody's eyes—and he didn't blame him. For a child Kaya's age, just starting her long academic slog, discouragement from a teacher could be crushing. The same thing had happened to Aaron when he was in first grade. Those kinds of scars stayed with you. Although he had to admit that Kaya seemed like a kid who wasn't afraid to speak her mind.

Aaron cleared his throat. "Kaya, Cody told you that I'm a historian, but I'm a librarian too. I love all kinds of books. Won't you show me yours?"

She tilted her head and gazed up at him, her huge brown eyes narrowed with suspicion. "A liberrian? Really?"

"Mmm-hmmm."

"Well. Okay, then." She took a deep breath, her narrow shoulders rising and falling, then opened the report almost reverently. Aaron felt a spike of his own anger. Clearly she'd been proud of this. It mattered to *her*, but her teacher had shot her down.

The first page had "Amelia Earhart" written in the shaky block letters of someone still practicing penmanship. The second page had a crayon rendering of a figure in a 1930s flight helmet. Although it was representational as only children's art could be, it was still recognizable as a female pilot.

"Amelia Earhart was born in Kansas. She liked basketball and cars. But her favorite thing was airplanes." Kaya turned the page to another picture of Earhart standing next to a bright yellow plane. "She called her very first plane the Canary because it was yellow like a canary."

"Really?" Aaron asked. "I didn't know that."

"Uh-huh." She turned the next page, which featured a plane dangerously close to very choppy bright blue water. "She did lots of things first. She was the first girl to fly across the Atlantic Ocean by herself." On the next page, the plane was aloft over a cornfield. "The first girl to fly across America by herself without stopping." Another page, this time with Earhart standing next to a woman in a grass skirt. "The first person, boy *or* girl, to fly from Hawaii to the rest of America. Then she decided she would fly around the world."

Aaron braced himself for what was coming next—the disappearance of Earhart and her copilot in the middle of the Pacific. But when she turned the page, the picture was of Earhart with a... kangaroo?

"And then she visited Australia."

"Um...."

Cody caught Aaron's gaze and shook his head. "What next?"

Kaya turned the page, revealing an obvious parade between tall buildings. "And when she got to New York, they gave her a parade." But Kaya wasn't done—there were still more pages to go. The next one showed Earhart

—still in her flight helmet—next to a tree with exuberant green leaves and dozens of red dots. "Then she went to Bishop's and picked apples with her family."

The next page showed Earhart in a rocking chair surrounded by a crowd of smaller figures with skin tones ranging from Earhart's peach to a brown slightly darker than Kaya's, all wearing pink high-tops and their own flight helmets. "And she had seven daughters and seven times seven granddaughters, and they all flew planes too. The end."

Cody tugged gently on the heavy braid that lay on Kaya's shoulder. "That's kind of a big family, don't you think?"

"No." Kaya closed the report and hugged it to her chest again. "History doesn't have enough girls in it. It should have more."

Aaron met Cody's gaze over Kaya's head and quirked an eyebrow. "You know, she's got a point."

Cody controlled his laughter because that wouldn't help Kaya one bit. "You know, munchkin—"

"Uncle Cody." The warning note in Kaya's voice was unmistakable. *Good.*

"You know, *kiddo*, that's not what really happened. Like we talked about when we were doing the research, Earhart's plane went down in the Pacific, and they never found her. She never made it to Australia, let alone New York or Bishop's."

Kaya had her dad's gorgeous brown skin and shiny black hair, but her determined chin and the expression on her face were 100 percent Eliza.

She sat back, nearly disappearing in the sofa cushions, her lower lip pushed out in a pout. "My ending was better."

"I agree. But it wasn't the assignment. Save the AU stuff for language arts."

She looked up at him from under lowered brows. "What's hey you?"

"Not 'hey you'—AU. Alternate Universe. Stories about the same people, but where different things happen to them."

"There are stories like that?"

"Sure. Lots of them."

She nodded decisively, her black bangs flopping on her forehead. "Then that's what I'm going to do when I grow up. I'm writing hey-you stories about all the stuff I don't like and make them end better."

"Careful, Kaya," Cody said, sharing a glance with Aaron. "Politicians do that all the time. They call it 'spin.'"

She pushed herself off the sofa. "I'm going to show Mommy and tell her about hey you."

Cody grabbed one of her hands. "Mommy's taking a nap right now, so think you could wait until she wakes up?"

"I suppose. This baby's kicking her in the butt."

Cody smothered his laugh. "Where did you hear that?"

She looked at him as if he were an idiot. "Mommy."

"Naturally."

Aaron's eyebrows rose above his glasses. "Baby?"

"Eliza's pregnant. Apparently it hasn't improved her disposition."

Kaya took a giant step to clear Cody's feet. "Okay. I'll go read it to Dexter."

"Dexter?" Aaron's half smile was almost more than Cody could resist.

"Cat. He's a tough critic. She probably got a better response from her teacher."

Hiran trudged back into the room, his normally smooth hair sticking out around his ears. "Sorry about that." He scanned the room. "Where's Kaya? She didn't do an end run to get to her mom, did she? Eliza's not feeling so great today."

"So I gather. According to Kaya, the baby's kicking her in the butt."

Hiran rolled his eyes. "I wish I could say it was an exaggeration. You were gone for her first pregnancy, so you don't remember, but she had morning-noon-and-night sickness for the first two trimesters, and it looks like the pattern is repeating. Your mom and dad are in Boston until tomorrow, visiting George, so I promised Eliza I'd keep Kaya occupied today, but...." He waved his phone. "The whole project team is imploding. I need to—" His phone rang again. "Sorry." He disappeared back into the kitchen as he answered it.

Aaron turned, resting his knee on the sofa to face Cody. "Is your sister a stay-at-home mom?"

"No. She's an architect in private practice. My parents are retired and I'm, you know, flexible, so between the three of us, we watch Kaya after school and on weekends when Hiran and Eliza are slammed."

Cody shifted uneasily on the too-soft cushions. If he left on the backpacking trip, what would that mean to his family? If Hiran was right—and he should know, since he'd been here—then not having Cody on deck to help out could be a huge problem. It sounded like Hiran needed help at the office too, and if Cody wasn't around to help with *that* either....

Today, though, he could totally step up to the plate.

Aaron had risen and was wandering around the room. "This is a great house."

"Thanks." He joined Aaron by the french doors. "I grew up here. It belonged to my mom and dad, but after Eliza and Hiran got married and I was off at college, they decided to downsize. By the time I got back from that sailing trip, Eliza had already planned and executed the renovation, so I moved into the attic apartment."

"So you're living in the house you grew up in."

He grinned. "Guilty. But at least I'm not still living in my old room with *Lord of the Rings* posters on the walls and shelves full of Star Wars action figures."

"No?"

"Nope. I'm living in the attic. With *Lord of the Rings* posters on the walls and shelves full of Star Wars action figures."

"Uh...."

"Kidding. The action figures are in storage."

Cody touched Aaron's arm, gratified when Aaron didn't flinch or pull away. "Look, I know I promised you a hike, but would you mind if we scaled it back a little and took Kaya with us? It'll give Hiran and Eliza a break, which sounds like they really need."

Aaron's smile warmed Cody down to his toes. "No, I don't mind."

"Great! We'll only be going about a mile and a half instead of what I'd planned, but the view is still spectacular, especially today. Clear, still a little cool, but it'll warm up by this afternoon in time for a posthike ice cream stop."

"Sounds like a plan." Aaron's brow knotted. "But is a six-year-old up for a three-mile hike?"

"Kaya? You bet. We're taking a lunch with us, so we'll have a break between going up and coming back down. Anyway, she's a tough little cookie. She goes on runs with me all the time."

He led Aaron into the kitchen where Hiran was stirring something on the stove—yellow curry sauce, by the mouthwatering aroma—while he talked in soothing tones into his phone.

He hung up and sighed. "I don't suppose I could talk you into hiring on full-time, Cody? These latest baby developers need their hands held for *everything*."

"Sorry. I'm not ready for that yet. But I can handle your immediate childcare issues. Aaron and I were planning on taking a long hike today, but we can change our plans. Head up to Sleeping Giant and take Kaya with us."

"Really?" Hiran's harried expression morphed into one of relief. "That would be outstanding. I could go in to the office and defuse the current project time bomb."

"You bet. We've got your back."

Aaron smiled. "Absolutely. I know what it's like to be up against a deadline and have no visible means of support."

"Thank you. I'll get her ready to go." Hiran's phone beeped again, and Cody laughed, clapping him on the back.

"Leave it to me. I'll talk her out of the pink high-tops and into her hiking boots before you can say 'revisionist history.'"

Hiran grasped Cody's shoulder in a firm grip. "You are a god among men, Cody Brown. I don't know what we'd do without you."

Cody would do anything for his family, any time, no questions asked. None of them ever took his effort for granted, which was nice and always gave him a warm fuzzy feeling. But the look on Aaron's face right then, that combination of admiration and longing?

It made him feel like a freaking superhero.

CHAPTER SEVEN

Aaron stared out the window, fascinated, as Cody drove through the New Haven streets. "You know, I'd heard about the Yale Art Gallery, but it looks even weirder in person. I mean a rectilinear windowed box grafted onto stone block gothic? It's like passive-aggressive conjoined twins with wildly different fashion sense."

"Yeah. Don't get Eliza started on that. She has *feelings.*" Cody glanced in the rearview mirror. "You okay back there, munchkin."

"Uncle Cody." Kaya looked up from her tablet to glare at him. "I *told* you."

"Yeah, yeah. Not a munchkin." He shot a mischievous glance at Aaron and mouthed *munchkin.* "You know," Cody said as he navigated the nest of one-way streets, "you're not the first person to run away to Connecticut."

Aaron returned to his rubbernecking, chest tightening. "I didn't run away."

"Dude. We already know you weren't running *to* something—at least not something concrete. Once you figured out which way was Connect-i-cut, you hopped on a plane and split."

Aaron sighed, drumming his fingers on his thigh. "Fine. I was running away. But when I saw Wayne picking out rings after refusing to consider the possibility with me.... Well, this camel's back wasn't strong enough for that particular straw."

"So you asked him to marry you and he turned you down?"

"No. I asked whether he'd ever thought about getting married, and he said never."

Cody turned another corner. "You realize that's not the same thing, right? Maybe he was waiting for you to pop the question so he *could* think about it?"

Aaron stopped drumming his fingers and gripped his knees instead. "How did we get on this subject?"

"We were talking about Connecticut as an escape hatch."

"Okay. I'll bite. Who else ran away to Connecticut?"

"Whalley, Goffe, and Dixwell."

Aaron turned in his seat and caught a smirk lifting Cody's lips. "Who?"

Cody scoffed. "And you call yourself a historian."

"Cut me a break." Aaron kept his tone tart, but the tension eased across his shoulders, as it always did under Cody's light-heartedness. "I've been researching kangaroos for the last month."

He waved one hand as if batting Aaron's words away. "Excuses. If you'd spent five minutes on *Connecticut* research before you ran, you'd know that Whalley, Goffe, and Dixwell were three of the regicide judges who signed Charles I's death warrant. When Charles II was crowned, England was suddenly a little too hot for them—as was Boston, where they first landed. They hid out here." He jerked his thumb to the left, toward an obviously busy—and very oddly configured—intersection. "In fact, three major streets in New Haven are named for them. We put up freaking *monuments* to them. We Connecticaners"—he stuck his nose in the air, putting on a fake posh accent—

"spit in the face of royal retribution. They—" Cody glanced in the back seat where Kaya was bobbing her head along to a song on her tablet. "Hmmm. Maybe we shouldn't be talking about them in front of her."

"We learned about them in *kindygarden,* Uncle Cody."

"You did?" He glanced in the rearview mirror again. "What do you think about them?"

Aaron swiveled around in his seat in time to see Kaya scrunch up her face, obviously deep in thought. "I think it's wrong to chop anyone's head off. But I *also* think it's wrong to change the rules after the game is already over." She turned her attention back to her tablet.

"Tough little cookie," Aaron murmured.

Cody chuckled. "Just wait until you meet my sister, and all will become crystal clear."

A little nugget of warmth lodged at the base of Aaron's throat, making it difficult to swallow. *He wants me around long enough to meet his sister. He's trusting me with his family.* Unable to speak, he looked out the window again as Cody drove them out of town and into the wooded hills.

"Here we go. Sleeping Giant State Park. So called because if you look at the silhouette of the hills from a certain perspective, it looks like a giant lying on his back."

Aaron cleared his throat, hoping his smile didn't look completely forced. *How often will you meet someone like this again? Don't waste the opportunity.* "You can say that about a lot of hill formations."

"Yeah, but we said it first. Come on."

They piled out of the car, Cody shouldering a backpack with their lunch.

"Sure I can't carry that for you?"

"You can carry it on the way back. How about that?"

"Seems hardly fair. It'll be lighter then."

"Just another one of my ploys to convince you that Connecticut is the place for you."

"Because people will carry my lunch for me?"

"Not just anybody. Only me."

Aaron smiled at the smug tone of Cody's voice. "You know, that's a pretty good enticement."

"Excellent!"

"Uncle Cody," Kaya called from the trailhead. "Are we hiking or not?"

"Right. Let's go."

They headed into the trees, the weather mild enough that all three of them had their jackets tied around their waists before they'd gone too far.

Cody had been right about the trail. It was probably way too easy for him, no problem for determined little Kaya, and not too much of a challenge for Aaron who'd spent most of his days lately behind a desk. He'd probably feel it in his calves tomorrow, but it would be worth it.

Because when they reached the pinnacle... *wow*. A 360-degree view spread out around them.

Cody was humming under his breath again. By now, Aaron had learned to pay attention, since the tunes were rarely random. Once he recognized this one, he started to chuckle. "The Who, right? 'I Can See for Miles.'"

Cody grinned. "Got it in one. Appropriate, though, right?"

"I'll say." Aaron turned slowly in a circle. "The scenery is gorgeous, yes, but I'm almost more impressed that I can *see* the scenery. I don't remember the last time the air was this clear in Santa Ana."

"Uncle Cody." Kaya was peering into the distance, where the skyline of a sizable city was clearly visible.

"Yeah, kiddo?"

"It takes us an hour to drive to Hartford."

"That's right."

She pointed to the city. "How come it doesn't take an hour to *see* Hartford?"

Cody opened his mouth, then snapped it shut. Aaron shared a raised-eyebrow gaze with him and shrugged. "I got nothin'."

Cody slung an arm across Kaya's shoulders. "That's a great question, but it's not something uncles are qualified to discuss. When you get home, you need to ask your mom and dad to explain it to you."

She screwed up her mouth in a moue of annoyance. "If you don't know, you could just *say* so."

He laughed. "Right. Sorry. Now what do you say to some lunch?"

Afterward, as he'd promised, Cody let Aaron cart the backpack down the hill to the parking lot. Aaron handed it off to him with a little bow, and Cody grinned before tossing it in the trunk.

He slammed the trunk shut and looked down at his niece. "You up for some ice cream, munchkin?"

Kaya stamped her foot. "Uncle *Cody!*"

Cody crouched down next to her, putting himself at her eye level. "If I take you to Ashley's for ice cream, can I call you munchkin then?"

She frowned in fierce concentration. "Not a stupid kid cone?"

"Nope. Full size. Double scoop. In a cup."

"Okay. But *only* when we're there. When we leave, you can't anymore."

"Deal."

As they sat in the ice cream parlor—which was apparently named for a Frisbee-playing whippet—Aaron tried desperately not to be mesmerized by the way Cody licked his ice cream cone with long, slow strokes of his tongue. *I'm in public, with a six-year-old, for pity's sake.*

He was not entirely successful, eating his own cup (bittersweet chocolate and rich enough to clog all his arteries at once) so fast that he gave himself an ice cream headache.

"So, Aaron," Cody said between licks. "I've got tomorrow off too. Since we did the mountains today—"

"I wouldn't call those *mountains*, precisely. More like hills."

"Hey, smaller state, smaller mountains. It isn't about size—it's about proportion."

Don't think about Cody's proportions. "I'll grant you that. Provisionally."

"So anyway, *mountains* today. How about ocean tomorrow?"

Aaron studied Cody's profile. *Lick.* Urgh. "You're not trying to entice me out on the ocean in a *boat*, are you?"

"I would never set sail with you—not until you're ready and ask me nicely."

From the twinkle in Cody's eyes—*lick*—he had something else up his sleeve, but Aaron was distracted enough—*lick*—that his guard was down.

"Okay. Ocean it is."

"And maybe river too. Bring swim trunks and a change of clothing."

"Uh...." He hadn't brought trunks with him. He wasn't even sure he still owned any. Lord, he lived within forty minutes of the beach, and he hadn't gone in years.

"It'll be fun. Trust me."

God help me. I do.

"Will they have ice cream where you're going when you take your trip this winter, Uncle Cody?"

Aaron glanced from Kaya, who was consuming her two scoops with fierce intensity, to Cody, who was suddenly very interested in a picture of Ashley Whippet catching a Frisbee midair.

"Are you going somewhere?"

"I... ah... sort of."

Kaya stuck her spoon in her ice cream and excavated an enormous bite. "He's going on a *really* long hike. Months and months and months."

"Months and months?" Aaron asked.

Cody scowled at his cone. "I'd like to know what Eliza was thinking, discussing it with Kaya when plans aren't finalized, but yeah. I was thinking of taking a solo backpacking trip this winter."

Cold spread from Aaron's belly—and not because of the ice cream. *He won't be here. If—no,* when—*the job comes through, I'll be just as alone as I was in California.*

The change in subject effectively ended the torture-by-ice-cream-cone. Cody helped Kaya finish her dish, and they trooped back to the car where Cody sang along with Kaya and her tablet—an upbeat song about pizza.

When they pulled into the driveway, Kaya ran inside ahead of them, already calling for her parents to ask them about how long it takes to see Hartford.

Aaron strolled up to the porch with Cody. "I had a great time today."

Cody grinned, and once again Aaron was nearly blinded by the glory. "Did you? You seemed a little distracted at Ashley's."

Aaron looked at him closely and detected a decided wicked edge to that grin. "You. You did that on purpose."

He widened his eyes and blinked them in mock innocence. "Who me?"

"Yes, you. Did you want me to embarrass myself in front of your niece?"

Cody sobered at once. "No, Aaron." He stepped closer, close enough that Aaron could feel the whisper of his breath on his cheek. "I would never want to embarrass you. But I want to do something else."

"What?" Aaron barely got the word out because his breath had gotten lost somewhere south of his throat.

"I want to kiss you. Is that okay?"

Aaron's voice got lost along with his breath, so he nodded.

Cody cradled Aaron's face in his hands and leaned forward, the soft press of his lips against Aaron's everything that heaven ever promised. Soft. Warm. Lush. Tasting slightly of lemon from his ice cream. But chaste. Aaron wasn't sure whether to protest or give thanks, because the excitement building in his belly and points south wanted *more more more*. But his common sense—that bastard—reminded him *You've only just met. He's a decade younger. Don't rush into things.*

But oh, Aaron wanted to rush. To rush and feel and *fall*.

Then Cody pulled away. "That was—" His laugh caught on a shaky inhale.

"That was what?"

"More than I expected? Everything I wanted? Not anywhere close to enough?"

Aaron stroked Cody's bright hair, so soft. "How about all of the above?"

"That works. I—"

"Uncle Cody!" Kaya stared up at them from the door. "Mommy says to get your butt inside. She has *words* for you."

"Be there in a sec, kiddo." Cody shared a rueful glance with Aaron. "I guess Eliza wasn't amused by my masterful sidestep."

"It was a pretty great dodge. Although I think your niece picked the wrong career."

"What?"

"She's not going to be a spec fic writer when she grows up. She's going to rule the world."

When Cody pulled up outside Aaron's Airbnb the next afternoon, Aaron was waiting at the curb, dressed in another polo-and-khaki ensemble, a leather messenger bag across his shoulder.

Cody hopped out to open the trunk. "Hey, you." Before it could get awkward, he pulled Aaron in for a quick kiss. Aaron's little *mmmph* of surprise made him worry that he'd misstepped, but when he drew back, Aaron was smiling, an adorable flush painting his cheeks.

"Hello to you too." He unslung his bag and tossed it in the trunk on top of Cody's blanket and towels. He frowned slightly, no doubt noting the absence of the picnic basket. "Do you need anything else? I have some snacks upstairs."

"Don't worry, Aaron. I won't let you starve. Everything's already been taken care of."

"That sounds ominous."

Cody gave him another quick peck and then slid behind the wheel. "I'd assume that a teacher would appreciate someone who prepares their assignments so conscientiously."

Aaron climbed in and buckled his seat belt immediately as he always did. "Am I an assignment, then?"

"No, doofus. Our date is an assignment—the next chapter in 'Introduce Aaron to the Awesomeness of Connecticut.'" He started the car. "Hey, speaking of teachers, have you heard anything from Hillview yet?"

"No. But it's Sunday. They said within the week, but I doubt they'd make a decision on the weekend anyway, right?"

Cody shrugged as he pulled out into traffic. "Hillview's a boarding school, so who knows? Sunday could be a part of their work week. But regardless, I'd say a longer wait is a good sign."

Aaron's lips quirked. "You would."

"What does that mean?"

"You're a glass half-full kind of guy."

"Pfft." Cody flicked his fingers. "Who needs glasses? Just use your hands or drink straight out of the hose, I always say." He grinned at Aaron's derisive snort. "But think about it. A longer wait means they're thinking about their choice. Deliberating. It's a fair process and not something that's rigged to comply with the letter of employment law."

"I suppose." Aaron sighed. "But it doesn't make the wait any easier."

"Well, I can do something about that." He patted Aaron's knee and was rewarded with a smile. "Sorry we had to start so late. I took pity on Hiran and untangled some code for him this morning."

"That quickly?"

Cody shrugged. "It wasn't that hard."

"Is that why he wants you to work for him?"

"That, and Hiran is a firm believer in nepotism. I think it may be a cultural thing. He always looks to family first."

Aaron was quiet for several minutes. When Cody glanced at him, he was staring out the window, and since the current scenery was nothing but strip malls and gas stations, it wasn't for the view.

"Everything okay?"

Aaron jerked slightly, as if he'd been miles away. "Yes. I'm just... thinking."

"Good thinking or bad thinking?"

Aaron glanced down at his lap. "Your family life is very different from mine."

"I think that's true for everybody. I mean what two families are the same?"

"Yes, but I'm talking about the atmosphere, the support, the security. As a kid, were you ever afraid that when you got home from school, you wouldn't have a home anymore?"

What? "No. That never entered my head, even though Eliza always threatened to convince our parents to move away whenever I left for camp."

"Well, it happened to me. More than once. My parents were... not responsible. I don't think 'stability' was anywhere in their vocabulary. Time and again, they'd gamble everything on the next golden opportunity—and although none ever panned out, it didn't stop them from believing that the next tip would be the one."

Cody gripped the steering wheel, knuckles whitening. "They gambled away your *home*?"

Aaron glanced at him quickly and then away again. "That would suppose that they had a home to begin with. We usually had a home *base* of sorts. Apartments mostly, a mobile home once, although that was a rental too. But sometimes it was just our car."

"Jesus, Aaron. With a kid? Why didn't they go to a shelter?"

"First, shelter beds are hard to come by, especially for a family that includes both parents. Second, they never tried. Shelters were for losers, as far as they were concerned, and even though they lost time and time again, they never put themselves in that category."

Cody muttered all the words he wasn't allowed to say in front of Kaya to himself as he took the turn onto Short Beach Road a little too viciously. "I know they were your parents, but I've got to say I think they were total assholes."

Aaron raised an eyebrow. "That doesn't sound like a niece-appropriate word."

"I don't care. They deserve it. They had a kid, for God's sake. *You* should have been their priority, not some pie-in-the-sky get-rich-quick scheme."

"Trust me," Aaron said, his tone dry, "you're not the only one with that opinion. My aunt finally stepped in when the living-in-a-car thing nearly got me sent into foster care. My parents hung around long enough to assign custody to her, then disappeared. I haven't seen them since I was ten."

Cody blinked, his throat thick. "I'm so sorry, Aaron. If it seems like I was, I don't know, *flaunting* my family in front of you, I didn't do it on purpose. If it upset you—"

Aaron gripped Cody's biceps, his fingers chilly against Cody's skin. "Don't ever think that. Just because I didn't have a perfect family life, it doesn't mean I begrudge other people theirs. Besides...." Aaron released him and leaned back in his seat.

"Besides what?"

Aaron's expression was somber, with those same sad eyes that had captured Cody's interest the first day. "I would hate to think of you being unhappy or frightened as a child."

Cody swallowed against a lump in his throat the size of a baseball as he turned onto Killams Point Road. "Thanks. You don't have to worry about that. My childhood was awesome, although while I was in it, I probably found plenty to complain about, just like any other self-centered kid. But I was never hungry or uncertain of my parents' love and support."

"Uh... Cody?" Aaron was staring out the window, craning his neck to look behind him. "That sign said this is private."

"It is. It belongs to my parents' church. They've got a conference center out here."

"Is it okay for us to be here?"

"Yes. Besides, my dad's a deacon. He can bail us out of religious trespassing jail if necessary."

"Cody—"

"Kidding." He glanced at Aaron's troubled face in the dappled light as they drove down the wooded road. "Do you *always* follow the rules?"

"Why? Do you think following the rules is somehow reprehensible?"

"Not reprehensible exactly. But I don't see the point in following arbitrary rules blindly. I mean, who's to say the rulemaker has the authority anyway? Don't you ever wonder why the rules are there?"

"No, I don't." Aaron's tone had a definite edge. "I wonder how many people died before somebody got off their ass and put the necessary safety regulations in place." Aaron huffed out a breath. "Sorry. Didn't mean go all dark side on you."

Cody patted his knee. "I'm telling you, Aaron, you need to find some more cheerful history. In fact, that's your homework. At our next date, you have to regale me with at least three stories—either events or people—that turned out well."

Aaron's lips quirked in a lopsided smile. "Regale you, huh?"

"Yes. I insist on being regaled. I don't think I've ever been regaled before. It'll be an adventure."

"You're assuming—I mean, will there be a next date?" Aaron's tone was tentative, as if he assumed Cody would hedge or outright deny the possibility.

"Are you asking what I want or trying to let me down easy?" Because Cody had heard it all before: *Flighty. Reckless. Adrenaline-junkie.* But despite his adventure lust, Cody would never put anyone else at risk—not their person and not their feelings. He parked the car along the side of the road, under the trees. "You know what I think?"

Aaron smiled wryly. "I'm afraid to ask."

"Then I'll tell you. You and me? We're serendipity."

"Isn't serendipity just another word for coincidence?"

"Yeah, but it's a *happy* coincidence, not doom-and-gloom destiny. Maybe it was garden-variety coincidence that you were standing in the middle of the Seaport green looking like an abandoned puppy—"

"I did not look like a puppy!"

"A *mournful* abandoned puppy, just as I was finishing my shift. But when you came back the next day—that wasn't coincidence. Yesterday wasn't coincidence. Neither is today. I'm telling you—serendipity. And we are totally rocking it." He leaned in to kiss the sad smile off Aaron's lips. "Are you... are you glad?"

Aaron ran the tip of one finger down Cody's cheek, eliciting a shiver. "Yes. Very glad. I'd go so far as to say thrilled. And as long as you don't drown me today, there will absolutely be a next date."

Cody laughed. "All righty, then. Let's hit the beach."

They walked through the trees to the narrow strip of sand bracketed by rocky outcroppings, the tiny waves of the Sound lapping at the shore.

Aaron looked around him with wonder. "This is a beach? That's the ocean?"

"Notice the sand." Cody spread his hands. "Notice the adjacent water. Definitely a beach. Although technically, it's the Long Island Sound. It's connected to the Atlantic, though. All you have to do is sail east for a bit and you're there."

Aaron turned in a slow circle. "The trees grow almost to the shore. And the water." He shook his head. "It's so calm, more like a lake."

"Trust me, things can get a lot wilder during a storm. But that's the advantage of the Sound, or of any kind of harbor really. The surrounding land protects it from nature's worst excesses."

"I guess I'm used to the way the public beaches in Southern California are always butted up against parking lots and overpriced real estate. And they're... um... a lot bigger and not nearly as empty."

"See? Even our beaches are a manageable size. Although this is a bit different because it's a private beach. The public ones can be larger and more populated." Cody kicked off his deck shoes and spread out the blanket, stacking the towels in the corner where they'd keep the blanket flat in the breeze. When he stood up, Aaron had removed his shoes and socks and rolled up his pant legs. "Seriously, Aaron? This is your idea of appropriate beachwear?"

Aaron shot Cody an exasperated glare. "Why would I have brought trunks? I was interviewing as a teacher, not a lifeguard. And last I checked, most libraries aren't located in a swimming pool." He balled his socks up and tucked them inside one of his shoes. "Anyway, you don't need to see me in all my fish-belly-white glory."

Cody waggled his eyebrows. "How do you know that isn't why I planned this whole thing? So I could see your fish-belly-white glory and revel in it?"

"So you're going to revel and regale?"

"*I'm* going to revel. The regaling is your responsibility."

"Well, as it happens, there can be no reveling because I don't have any trunks with me."

"Aha. You have reckoned without your host."

Aaron smiled. "So now we're reckoning as well as reveling and regaling? Have you been reading the RE section of the dictionary as light bedtime fare?"

"Nope. Strictly serendipity. I'd ask you to skinny-dip, but this is a *shared* private beach, so you never know who else from the church might show up." Cody stuck his hand between the towels and pulled out a second pair of trunks. "*Voilà!*"

Aaron burst out laughing. "I'm impressed. However, I think I'll stick to wading anyway. That's the most I've ever done in the Pacific. I wouldn't want it to feel slighted."

"All right. I won't push." *See? I'm learning. I can let him set his own comfort-zone limits.*

Cody stripped off his T-shirt and tossed it on his towel. When he looked up, Aaron was staring at his chest. When Aaron licked his lips, Cody's cock perked up and said *Hello, sailor.* Yikes!

He turned and splashed into the water. Even though the Sound was shallow here, the water was still *cold*—which was exactly what Cody needed to avoid embarrassing himself. He stopped when the water reached midthigh, though, because he didn't want his balls to retract completely.

"When we were kids, my folks used to bring us down here to go clamming. We've brought Kaya down since she could toddle."

Aaron strolled along the surf line, the wavelets occasionally foaming around his toes. "I take it she's not afraid of the water."

"Are you kidding? I think she's half fish." Cody dug his toes into the sand. "Hold on. I think I've found one."

"One what?"

"A clam."

"You can find clams with your feet?"

"Sure. Using a rake is unsporting. I figure this way, the clams have an equal chance." He held up his hands, fingers spread. "At least until I bring opposable thumbs into the picture." He bent over, plunging his hand into the water and came up with a handful of dripping sand.

"Impressive."

"Don't be a smartass." He swished his hand through the water and displayed a shellfish in his palm with a grin. "There. Steamer."

Aaron's eyes rounded in horror. "What the hell is *that*?"

Cody touched the fleshy protuberance at one end of the shell. "That's its feeding tube."

"It's kind of—"

"Sci-fi freaky? Yeah, they've always reminded me of the face-hugger in *Alien*."

"Actually, my take was less PG."

Cody held the clam up between two fingers. "Heh. Guess they are a little lewd. Stick with me, baby. I'm *all* about the shellfish porn." He flung it over his shoulder with a flourish, and it plopped back in the water.

Aaron laughed again, a much freer sound than Cody had heard from him before. He gazed out at the horizon. "This is wonderful. And the weather is lovely."

Cody waded onto shore. "I'm afraid you're getting a skewed idea of our weather." He walked over and collapsed onto the blanket, patting the spot next to him in invitation. "This is my favorite time of year actually.

Warm but not hot, days are still longer than nights, at least for a few more weeks, but the trees are starting to get sleepy. Yeah, between Labor Day and peak leaf season in the middle of October, when it starts to get colder? It's the best."

"You're not filling me with confidence here." Aaron sat down gingerly, keeping his wet, sandy feet off the edge of the blanket. "What's so bad about the rest of the time?"

"Oh, that's right." Cody added a snooty drawl to his tone. "You So Cal people don't have *seasons*."

"We have seasons."

"Really?" Cody lay back and laced his hands behind his head, warm from the sun and from the heat of Aaron's gaze. "How can you tell? If you look out your window in June, how is it different from the same view in January? Or October?"

"Easy. By whether the women are wearing their Uggs with shorts or leggings, and whether the guys are wearing tanks or T-shirts."

Cody chuckled. "Don't get me wrong. I like our other seasons too. Every month has something to recommend it. Except maybe February. February always sucks. Luckily, it's short."

Aaron smiled down at him, the sun glinting off his glasses, and for a moment, Cody's chest tightened with such tenderness and affection that he could barely breathe.

He took a shuddering breath and blurted, "I have a confession to make."

Aaron's smile faded, the now-familiar half-fearful expression creeping back onto his face. *Damn it. I hate that.* "I'm afraid to ask."

"I've concealed certain aspects of this date from you."

Aaron proceeded to give Cody a frankly appraising glance that took him in from chest to sandy toes. "I'm not sure where you could conceal anything in that outfit."

Erp. Including his rather noticeable reaction to Aaron's once-over. "Mind out of the gutter, Mr. Historian. I'm talking about dinner."

"Are you taking me to another restaurant with a misleading name?"

"Not exactly."

"Well then, what?"

"I'd rather show you than tell you. Are you ready to go?"

Aaron gestured to Cody's sand-covered extremities. "I'm not sure I'm the one who needs to answer that."

Cody waved the question away. "My car can stand a little sand. It's handled worse." He stood and offered a hand to Aaron. "Let's hit the road."

Aaron took his hand, and when Cody pulled him to his feet, he exerted a little too much force—or else Aaron didn't need quite as much help—because they were chest to chest, faces inches apart, close enough that Cody could see the dark rim around Aaron's blue irises.

His breath sped up, and his cock, which was already in a *Yeah, baby!* mode, got more insistent. No way was Cody having sex *here*, no matter what his genitals had in their heads. But kissing. Yeah. He could do that. They'd broken that particular ice a couple of times already, hadn't they?

"Hi," he murmured.

"Good afternoon." Aaron's smile was an invitation that Cody didn't care to resist.

He started to close the distance, but Aaron beat him to it, taking Cody's lips, pressure and warmth and a hint of tongue, his fingers threading deep into Cody's hair.

Cody moaned and wrapped his arms around Aaron's waist. *Damn this polo. I want skin.*

But when his knees started to buckle, he remembered. *Public private beach. A* church group *public private beach.*

He pulled away with a gasp.

Aaron let go immediately. "Sorry. I'm sorry. I shouldn't have—"

"Hey. I'm totally glad you made another leap. It's just...." Cody gestured to the water and the trees and the sky. "Not private. And sex on the beach is *not* what it's cracked up to be."

"Sex? Are we... are we headed there?"

"I sure hope so. But only if you're okay with it."

"*God* yes."

"Well then, hold that thought, because the day isn't over yet."

CHAPTER EIGHT

Although Aaron's brain was still in a lust-induced haze, he couldn't mistake what he was looking at.

"Cody. That's a boat."

Cody grinned at him, his cheeks pinked by the afternoon in the sun and his wavy hair mussed by the breeze. Well, the breeze and Aaron's fingers, if he were honest. Everything about Cody was so incredibly enticing that Aaron wanted to kiss him again.

Except... a boat.

"Yep. However, you'll note that it's somewhat more advanced than the *Morgan*." Cody climbed aboard, standing between the two wheels at the stern—*why the heck are there two steering wheels anyway?* "Fossil fuel backup. Electronic navigation and communication equipment. The galley has a microwave, the head has a shower, and the cabin sleeps four."

"Four? Are we expecting a crew to join us?"

"No, doofus. I'm just trying to reassure you about the amenities. Also, please note, we are docked. In a river." He gestured to the familiar grounds behind him. "At the historic Mystic Seaport. It's a calm night. No clouds. In other words, you are in no danger of drowning or being lost at sea." He held out his hand. "Welcome aboard, Mr. Templeton. Your dinner awaits."

When Cody put it that way, the butterflies dive-bombing Aaron's insides seemed ridiculous. He took

Cody's hand and stepped in, tensing for a moment when the boat dipped under his weight.

"Steady there. She's just adjusting to you." The cockpit had wood-slatted benches on either side of a central drop-leaf table. "Won't you please be seated? Port or starboard, your choice."

Port, left. Starboard, right. I at least know that much nautical terminology. Aaron sat down gingerly as Cody pulled a beer bottle out of a storage locker under the table. He pried the top off the bottle with an opener mounted under the table edge and presented it to Aaron with a flourish and a wink. "Your first drink of the evening, sir."

Aaron chuckled as he accepted it. *Might as well get into the spirit.* "Ah, thank you, garçon. A very fine vintage."

"The best. And may I offer you an hors d'oeuvres?" He produced a covered dish from the same storage area, whisking the lid off to display several dozen pretzels, garnished with a sprig of parsley.

Aaron took one. "I see you haven't exaggerated the amenities of this… er… noncruise."

Cody laughed and set the pretzels the table. "This is just to occupy you. I need to go below and get cleaned up. The rest of our dinner—our real dinner—is down there."

"Have you added magician to your other skills? How did you manage this?"

"This is my aunt and uncle's boat. I asked my cousin Kenny to sail it over here while we were at the Point."

"But docking here, at the Seaport?"

"It's totally a thing. People do it all the time, so don't imagine I had to pull any strings. Or not many anyway." He leaned down and kissed Aaron. "I'll be back in ten minutes. Don't go away." He disappeared below deck.

Aaron leaned back, nibbling on the pretzel, the peace of the deepening twilight doing nothing to ease his thrumming nerves. *Sex. I'm going to have sex tonight.* He wasn't entirely sure he was ready for the nakedness—both physical and emotional—that sex implied. After all, he hadn't slept with anyone but Wayne for years, and he obviously hadn't met *those* expectations.

I've known Cody for four days. How could the need to please him become so necessary so fast? Aaron didn't leap into relationships any quicker than he made any other decision. It had taken Wayne a solid month to talk him into a date. *Maybe that was because I knew we didn't really fit.*

But did he fit with Cody? Cody was fearless and unselfconscious, secure in the love of his family and for his home. Aaron was… not.

But maybe, with him, I could be.

A new job. A new home. A new relationship. It could work. And it filled him with a joy and contentment that in no way diminished his excitement or his apprehension.

Cody reappeared, halfway up the companionway steps. With his wet hair combed back against his head, he reminded Aaron of some sleek sea creature—and he looked absurdly young.

He held out a large metal bowl. "Hey, can I hand off the salad to you?"

Aaron scooted along the bench until he could stand, careful not to whack his head on the boom, and took the bowl. "Looks great. Not an iceberg wedge in sight."

Cody scrunched his nose. "Please. Iceberg is not lettuce. It's a conspiracy by the military-industrial complex. Or maybe an invading alien species." He backed down the steps, humming something that Aaron finally recognized as "Feed Me, Seymour" from *Little Shop of Horrors.*

A moment later he returned and passed Aaron a stack of white ceramic bowls, a couple of rolled-up cloth napkins, and a trivet made of wine corks. "I hope you're not one of those hoity-toity types who insists on china, crystal, and sixteen different kinds of forks all laid out on spotless linen."

Aaron arranged the new items on the table. "Usually I insist on Royal Doulton and antique silver for my salad and pretzels, but if I must, I'll make an exception tonight."

"Keep your socks on, smart guy. I'm not done yet."

He vanished again, then returned wearing anchor-print oven mitts and lugging a steaming pot of something redolent of thyme and onion. "This noncruise isn't upscale enough for lobster, but we're keeping with the seafood motif since we're, you know, on the sea. Ish." He set the pot on the trivet and shucked off the mitts. "You were introduced to the primary ingredient of tonight's main course this afternoon." He ladled a generous portion into one of the bowls and nudged it toward Aaron. "Specialty of the house... er... ship. Clam chowder."

Aaron inhaled the steam curling up from the soup. "It smells fabulous, but I've never seen it with a clear broth before."

"It's Rhode Island style." Cody waved a hand. "I know, I know. Not exactly in keeping with our Connecticut theme, but it's the kind I grew up on. George, my brother, was lactose intolerant as a kid, and Eliza hated tomatoes as ingredients for anything except ketchup."

"So that ruled out Manhattan style as well as New England?"

"Yup. But we all loved clams and used to fight about whose turn it was to have *their* kind of soup, so my parents got this recipe as a survival measure."

Aaron tasted a spoonful. "It's delicious. Did you make it?"

Cody chuckled. "Not this time. Too busy untangling Hiran's spaghetti code. Although to be fair, it was his new developer's code, not his. No, I begged this from my dad."

Aaron's chest tightened. *Family again.* "That was... really nice of him."

"He's a nice guy, but it wasn't a hardship. Whenever he makes this, he always makes the same vast quantity that he used to when all three of us kids were still living at home, even though he's only cooking for him and Mom now. He *claims*—" Cody set the word off with air quotes. "—that it doesn't taste the same if he tries to scale it down. So whenever he's in a chowder mood, Eliza and I don't have to stress about dinner plans."

"In other words, I shouldn't feel special?"

Cody raised his gaze from his bowl and grinned. "Oh, you're definitely special. I don't share this with just *anybody*." He snapped his fingers. "Hold on. I forgot the bread." He scampered below again, returning with a crusty baguette. "This is a rip-off-a-chunk kind of loaf, if you don't mind."

"I think it's all perfect. So why don't you sit down and enjoy it with me."

Cody grinned. "Don't mind if I do." He collected a beer for himself and instead of flipping up the other table leaf and sitting on the opposite bench, he slid in next to Aaron. Their hips brushed, and Aaron could smell the clean scent of Cody's skin and a hint of herbal soap despite the savory aroma of the soup.

They ate for a while in a silence that felt comfortable, not strained, the quiet village in front of them, the river behind, and the stars winking in above.

"This is nice."

Cody cocked his head, scanning the row of buildings nearest them. "I know. It looks different when there's nobody around. I mean, I love it during the day when it's busy and full of people. But I think I like it best like this. Quiet. Serene. Secret, almost."

"I get it. Way back in the day when I worked at Disneyland—"

"Thousands and thousands of years ago?" Cody's voice had a teasing edge.

"Don't exaggerate. It was well after the first Continental Congress. Anyway, in the summer, the park sponsored employee canoe races around Tom Sawyer's Island. My stand fielded a team, and I got talked into joining it."

"Oho!" Cody crowed. "So you *have* been on an undocked boat before!"

Aaron rolled his eyes. "A canoe on a man-made river barely a hundred feet wide and eight feet deep at most. That's not the point."

"Sorry." Cody smiled. "Not sorry."

"Yeah, okay. Anyway, the practices and races were really early in the morning, before the park opened. And since it opened at 8:00 in the summer, that meant 5:30, 6:00."

Cody winced. "Oooh. Rough."

Aaron shrugged. "Not really. I'm kind of a morning person. Anyway, walking through the empty park, right after dawn, when the light is pink and the streets are still wet from being washed down? It was special. How many people ever get to see that?"

Cody leaned into him, pressing their arms and shoulders together. "I get it. You were part of the family."

"Yeah. Yeah, I guess I was."

Another boat passed by on the river, its wake sending their boat rocking gently.

"Does this boat have a name? I hate to keep thinking about it as 'the boat.'"

"It does. *Nancy's Fancy II.*"

"Was there a *Nancy's Fancy I*?"

"Yes. My aunt's name is Nancy, and my uncle bought the first boat for their tenth anniversary, then replaced it with this one on her last birthday."

"Is your whole family obsessed with boats?"

Cody cast him a sidelong glance as he spooned a mouthful of chowder. "Not obsessed. But when you live in a coastal town, it's kind of a no-brainer. I mean, the water is *right freaking there.* Why wouldn't you go out on it?"

"Extending the area of your 'manageable-sized' state?"

"Maybe." He gestured expansively with his spoon. "Nothing like a little maritime elbow room. Although sometimes it can get a little more extensive than you plan."

Aaron sopped up some broth with a hunk of bread. "What do you mean?"

"Since the Connecticut shoreline is all along Long Island Sound, that's where you spend your time in the summer if you've got a boat. But there are no docks on the Sound. So if you're planning to spend a summer weekend on your boat, usually you anchor it in the Sound and use a smaller craft to go back and forth from shore." He set his empty bowl down and stretched his arm along the rail behind Aaron's back.

"I take it *Nancy's Fancy I* and *II* have such crafts?"

"Yep. Same one, in fact—a pretty basic plywood dinghy. I mean, it doesn't have to be elaborate to row back and forth from shore. Anyway, Uncle John allowed Kenny and me to mess around in the dinghy when we were kids. One day while we were rowing around, we spotted a tree floating in the Sound and thought, in typical meddling boy fashion, 'Hey, let's go mess around with *that.*'"

Aaron set his own bowl aside, the excellent dinner suddenly sitting uneasily in his stomach. "How old were you?"

Cody squinted up at the starry sky. "I was probably around ten, and Kenny was thirteen, maybe fourteen. Anyway, we started rowing. And rowing. And rowing. It took way longer to reach the damn tree than we expected. What we didn't realize was that as we were rowing toward it, it was moving away. By the time we finally got to it, we were almost out of sight of land."

Aaron gripped his knees and tried to keep his breathing steady. "Were you in the ocean?"

"Not quite. We started rowing back, but the current was taking us sideways from where we wanted to go, so we decide to just get to land somewhere and find our way back to Madison afterward."

"Is that what...." Aaron croaked. He cleared his throat. "Is that what you did?"

Cody chuckled. "We tried. But Dad and Uncle John had called the Coast Guard on us. We got towed back to the river dock. Kenny's always said that the sight of my dad standing there with his arms crossed, scowling like a WWE wrestler, was more frightening than the thought of drowning."

Cody started whistling "The Wreck of the Edmund Fitzgerald," and Aaron's control broke.

He leaped to his feet, fists clenched, and faced Cody, who was staring at him with his mouth agape.

"It's not *funny*, Cody. It's not something to joke about with theme music and a fucking *laugh track*." Aaron's breath sawed in and out. "You could have *died*." Heat surged behind Aaron's eyes, threatening to spill over. He turned away, striding between the dual wheels to stand at the stern, staring out at the dark river.

"Hey." Cody's voice was barely louder than the lap of water against the hull. "I'm sorry. I didn't tell you that to upset you." He rested his chin on Aaron's shoulder. "It worked out okay. Kenny and I are both still causing our dads grief. Think of it as history that had a cheerful outcome. Well, cheerful in that we made it back to shore. Not so cheerful in terms of what our punishment was. We spent the rest of that summer—and the next one too—scraping barnacles off *all* our parents' friends' boats rather than setting foot on our own."

Aaron whirled to face him. "You don't get it. You could have *died*."

Cody's brow was knotted with concern. "I was there, Aaron. Of course I get it. But there's no point in freaking out about it now. It's past and I'm here now. I'm fine."

Aaron traced Cody's face with trembling fingers. "You could have *died*." His voice broke, but he was done talking. He crushed his mouth to Cody's, a desperate mashing of lips, a clash of teeth, an awkward swipe of tongue, whimpering because this wasn't about seduction or romance or *pleasure*—it was about fucking proof of life.

But after a moment, Cody's solid presence, his chest warm against Aaron's, his scent, his stubble rasping against Aaron's lips, and the pressure of his palms on Aaron's back, penetrated Aaron's fog of panic.

He pulled back, resting his forehead against Cody's. "Sorry. I'm sorry, I shouldn't have—"

"You absolutely should." Cody continued to stroke Aaron's back. "You've told me, Aaron. You've told me more than once and in more than one way that safety and security are important to you, and that you're not comfortable with the ocean. I should have known that story would be a trigger."

"You don't have to make allowances for my neuroses."

"Why not? It's part of being a worthwhile human being, isn't it, to be considerate of other people's feelings? Even if the story weren't an issue, I shouldn't have been so flip about it." He stroked Aaron's hair. "Really. I'm the one who's sorry."

"Don't be." Aaron took a deep breath. "Cody, you are light and joy, and I would never want you to be any different. But the idea that all of that could have been snuffed out before I had a chance to meet you. Before the world had a chance to meet you. Before your *niece* had a chance to meet you. Well, that was a trigger for sure. But that's on me, not you. For now...."

Cody's eyes were darker than the river. "For now?"

Aaron leaned in and pressed a tender kiss to Cody's lips, then took his courage in both hands. "For now, I would really like to make love with you."

"That...." Cody swallowed, his mouth gone dry as hardtack. "That can be arranged."

Aaron's smile glimmered in the glow from the Village's safety lights. "Naturally. My Mystic man thinks of everything."

Cody took Aaron's hand and led him to the companionway. "Watch your step—and your head. You're a bit taller than any of our other passengers. I'll go first."

Below deck, Cody led him across the salon to the wide bed in the bow. His skin felt as if he'd plugged himself into the nearest outlet. Sure, he'd hoped they'd end up here when he'd planned the day, but he hadn't expected it to be this... momentous.

This *mattered*. No way could he escape with zero consequences. *But I'm not sure I'd want to escape anyway.* "As you can see," he said, attempting to defuse his own nerves with his best cruise director impression, "our accommodations are much more luxurious than the *Morgan*."

Aaron nodded, rubbing his thumb over the back of Cody's hand in a *very* distracting manner. "Yes. Very nice. The noticeable absence of harpoons is appreciated too."

"Well...." Cody quirked an eyebrow and let his glance stray to Aaron's groin. "I wouldn't say a *complete* absence of harpoons."

Aaron blinked, his jaw dropping, then broke into laughter. "You are an adventure all on your own." He crowded Cody against the storage closet door, pressing their bodies together. "An adventure I'd never have taken if I hadn't.... If I hadn't—"

"Leaped?"

He grinned. "Exactly." He dipped his head and kissed Cody's neck, then nuzzled the angle of his jaw. "You smell like the sea. Clean and salty and more than a little bit wild."

Cody's breath hitched, as if it couldn't make its way up his rib cage. "Is that a bad thing?"

"No." Aaron inhaled, long and slow. "I think I'm becoming addicted." He looked down into Cody's eyes. "To your scent, to your spirit. To your... feet."

Cody gasped out a laugh. "My feet?"

"You have very sexy feet," Aaron murmured. Then he pulled back, his expression suddenly morphing from sultry to apologetic. "Not that I have a foot fetish or anything. Not that there's anything *wrong* with that, if that's what you're into—"

"Aaron. It's okay. I don't think you're a sex maniac."

Aaron laughed shakily. "Thank God." He smoothed Cody's hair back from his forehead. "However, I do need to mention that the sight of your bare chest today engendered some very... er... sex maniacal thoughts."

"Yeah? In that case...." Cody pulled his T-shirt over his head. "I'm all over that."

"*Oh.*" Aaron swallowed, his Adam's apple sliding in a way that made Cody want to take a bite. "I haven't done this with anyone for a while." His fingers trembled as his hands settled on Cody's hips, sending Cody's heart into full-on overdrive.

"You're doing pretty good for being out of practice, then."

Aaron stilled, a smile blooming. "Really?" He leaned in until his lips were a breath from Cody's own. "Tell me what's on your mental playlist right now, and I'll tell you whether I believe you."

"Playlist?" Cody licked his lips, his tongue encountering the corner of Aaron's mouth. *Ungh!* "Taiko drums, I think."

Aaron pressed his hand in the center of Cody's chest and whispered against Cody's lips. "I think that's your heartbeat."

"Aaron," Cody whispered.

"Mmmm?" His lips vibrated against Cody's.

"If you don't kiss me now, I'll show you what maniacal *really* looks like."

"I wouldn't want that."

This time Aaron's kiss wasn't the frantic thing it had been up on deck. It started out sweet and soft, as if he was exploring all the ways their mouths could fit together—and there seemed to be a lot more than Cody had ever encountered in the past. *Thank God for librarians. They really know how to research!*

Aaron's research into all the ways he could make Cody moan with his tongue took him farther south—*neck, shoulder, pec,* nipple! *Gah!*

"This... is... *nnngh...* so unfair."

"What is?" Aaron murmured against Cody's skin, adding a little nip that caused Cody's hips to jerk forward, seeking heat and friction.

"I'm half-naked, but you're still wearing a damn polo and chinos."

Aaron glanced up at him. "A fair point. Plus—" He stood up, pressing a hand to his lower back. "—my back can't take this position for much longer."

"I could point out that the berth is right behind you."

Aaron glanced over his shoulder. "So it is." He looked back at Cody. "Your noncruise has so many fascinating immersive activities that I'd forgotten."

"We include a turn-down service, you know." Cody tugged Aaron's shirttail out of his pants.

"Indeed? And apparently a valet on staff as well."

"Well, this *is* an all-inclusive noncruise." Unable to wait another instant, Cody lifted Aaron's shirt over his head, being careful not to dislodge his glasses. In the dim light from the ports and overhead hatch, Aaron's skin glowed like cream, and Cody sucked in a breath.

Aaron glanced down at his chest and winced. "Fish-belly white."

"And here I am...." Cody skated his fingers from Aaron's collarbone, down his chest, and around his ribs. "Reveling."

"Is reveling a part of this noncruise too?"

"Like I said." He unbuckled Aaron's belt, then stepped away, shucking his own shorts and briefs down his legs. "All-inclusive." He climbed onto the bed and scooted back to lie down against the pillows, spreading his arms.

Aaron licked his lips. "Damn. If I'd known shipboard life was like *this*...." He shed his own pants, his long, cut cock standing proud in a nest of sandy curls, then crawled onto the bed, prowling forward on hands and knees until he was looming over Cody. "Permission to come aboard?"

Cody laced his fingers behind Aaron's neck. "Granted." He pulled Aaron down. When their lips met, Aaron sighed and lowered himself until they were touching, skin to skin, *aallll* the way down.

This. Him. Cody tightened his arms around Aaron, blood heating as the kiss deepened. *He's anchor and safe harbor, all in one.*

CHAPTER
NINE

The stupid seagulls crying outside woke Cody at dawn. After a lifetime spent near the shore, he ought to be used to them by now, but he'd never managed to tune them out. It hadn't been that much of an issue when he was a kid and was eager to get out on the water, or on a sail, when he was ever popular for taking the early-morning watch. Today, though? It was just criminal.

Because a warm, sleeping Aaron nestled in the pillows next to him, his pale, freckled back like a reverse star field. Cody spooned closer, nuzzling his nape, playing with the hair on Aaron's chest.

"Mmmm." Aaron captured Cody's hand, lacing their fingers together. "Apparently this noncruise includes a wake-up service too."

Cody kissed him between his shoulder blades. "We take our all-inclusivity *very* seriously."

"Then allow me to lodge a request for a bigger bathroom. I banged my elbows on every available surface in there." He patted Cody's hand and rolled to a sitting position. "And I'm about to repeat the abuse."

While Aaron was in the head, Cody stretched, enjoying the tiny post-sex discomforts—like beard burn on his face, throat, and inner thighs—that reminded him of what he and Aaron had done for most of the night. No doubt Aaron could catalog an identical set of sensations—in addition to his elbow bruises.

It had been... *magical.* Sometimes messy, occasionally awkward, but magical nonetheless.

Cody couldn't wait to do it again.

Aaron emerged from the head, and even though he'd put his boxer briefs back on, without his glasses he somehow looked more naked. He blinked in the crepuscular light as if he couldn't figure out why he wasn't able to focus.

Cody snagged his glasses off the headboard and held them out. "Here. This might make it easier to navigate."

"Thanks." He settled them on his nose. "I didn't think it was possible."

"What?"

"You're gorgeous even at the ass-crack of dawn."

The heat spreading across Cody's chest and up his throat meant he was in the throes of another stupid full-body blush. He could probably be mistaken for one of the lobsters at The Place. For crying out loud, when had he become self-conscious about his looks? *Since it matters that someone specific finds them attractive.*

Aaron ducked to peer out the port at the sunrise, scratching his jaw absently, so Cody pulled the sheet up over his chest and *reveled* in the sight of Aaron's body.

Yes, Aaron's skin was pale, and although he disparaged it as *fish-belly white*, to Cody, it was nothing short of mouthwatering. Then he noticed a dark pattern curling around Aaron's ribs above his hip.

"Hey. You have ink. How did I miss that last night?"

"Minimal ink." Aaron flashed a grin. "And you were busy reveling in the fish-belly white, so perhaps it escaped detection." He glanced down at himself. "This is the tattoo I got the night after I graduated with my MLS, the night I met Wayne. It gave him a false impression of my bad-boy quotient, poor man."

"Don't spare any sympathy for him. He's an idiot." Cody scooted forward, keeping the sheet over his lap, so he could examine the tattoo up close and personal. It was a rectangular frame about the size of his palm, with a scrollwork border and a Latin inscription. "Is it a bookplate?"

Aaron winced, rubbing the back of his neck. "Yeah. It was supposed to just say 'Ex Libris,' but I was a little drunk, so I didn't trust myself to describe what I wanted. I gave the bookplate to the tattoo artist so he could copy the words, but apparently my instructions were a little vague. Instead, he copied the whole thing, including the border." He smiled crookedly. "I wondered why it took so freaking long to ink."

"Doesn't 'Ex Libris' mean 'from the library of' somebody or other? Why is it blank?"

Aaron chuckled. "I wasn't *that* drunk. Besides at the time, I guess you could say I was still in circulation. Didn't belong to anybody."

Cody's throat thickened, a sudden wave of want washing over him. *You do now.* But that was stupid. They'd known each other less than a week. *Sometimes that's all it takes.*

Eliza had met Hiran at a party that she wasn't even supposed to be at—she'd missed her train home and got cajoled into going to the party by her college roommate. She'd always said that one look was all it took for her to know he was the one, even if it took her another year and a half to convince him. Cody's parents had met at a wedding and six months later were married themselves.

In fact, when he thought about it, love at first sight was a *tradition* in his family. Who was he to fight the inevitable? *But Aaron doesn't leap. I'll just have to exercise patience until he realizes he's hooked, and then I'll reel him in.*

"Are you hungry? I can fix breakfast. Or we could just laze around for a while longer."

"What kind of breakfast does your noncruise run to? Are we talking a full English," Aaron said, putting on a faux-British accent, "or merely a continental?"

"Actually, we're talking coffee, OJ, and toasted bagels with cream cheese."

Aaron grinned. "Works for me. I'll get dressed and go up on deck to stay out of your way. Your noncruise may be rich in certain amenities, but space is not one of them."

"It'll be chilly up there. Take the blanket off the bench in the salon. You'll enjoy the scenery much more if you're not shivering. I'll bring the coffee up as soon as it's done."

Aaron bent down to deliver a toe-curling kiss. "Don't be long. I've discovered I enjoy the scenery much more when you're part of it."

The rising sun tinged the quaint cottages of the Seaport orange-pink as Aaron sat in the cockpit, wrapped in a soft fleece blanket that smelled like Cody. The boat bobbed just a little, but he'd gotten used to it overnight. In fact, he hadn't slept so well in a long time. *Since well before Wayne left.*

Like the boat, he was floating, borne up on a sea of contentment that he'd never felt before. Even after his aunt had rescued him from his parents' substandard childrearing practices, he'd never achieved anything more than a manageable equilibrium. This tranquility, this welling joy, was something new.

He inhaled deeply, the salt tang of the sea so different from the smog-laden air of home. *No, not home. Not anymore.*

But this morning, instead of sending panic racing through his veins, the reminder was actually liberating. Nothing remained to tether him to his old life. He was free to set sail on this new one, in a new place, with a new man who was already firmly anchored in his heart.

His phone vibrated in the pocket of his jacket. He frowned as he untangled his arms from the blanket. Who in the world would be calling at this time? It was barely six. His heart stuttered when caller ID flashed Hillview.

He nearly fumbled the phone but managed to swipe the screen to answer the call. "Hello?"

"Oh, Mr. Templeton." Dr. Kensington's tone held surprise and—was that dismay? "I'm sorry. I expected to simply leave you a message to set a time to chat later."

"That's all right. I'm an early riser."

"Yes. Well." He cleared his throat. "I wanted to tell you how much the staff and students enjoyed your presentation. You clearly have a lot to offer any school lucky enough to have you."

Butterflies fluttered against Aaron's ribs. *This is it. I've got the job.* "Thank you."

"However, we've decided to go with another candidate."

Aaron's heart tumbled to his feet. "I... I understand." *But I don't. Not really. What did I do wrong?* "Do you mind sharing any of your reasons? Anything that might make my next attempt more successful?"

"It really wasn't anything to do with you. All three candidates were eminently qualified. However, the committee decided that retaining the instructor who's been filling the position on an interim basis would be less disruptive for our students."

"I... I see. Well." Aaron's throat closed up, making the last word come out as a croak. "Thank you for the opportunity in any case."

"I meant what I said, Mr. Templeton. You would clearly be an asset to any institution."

But not yours. "I appreciate it."

"We wish you all the best. Goodbye."

Aaron sank down on the bench, staring the phone long after Dr. Kensington ended the call. His fingers had gone numb, and he started to shiver in the crisp morning air.

I have no job. I have no home. I'm three thousand miles away from everything I know. "What the *fuck* am I doing? What the *fuck* was I *thinking?*" He knew better. He *knew* what happened when you didn't have your safety net in place, and yet he'd blithely assumed he was exempt this time.

His breath came in gasps, uncertainty opening a pit in his middle big enough for him to fall into and disappear.

"Hey, I was thinking." Cody's tone was cheerful as ever as he rose up the companionway steps, carrying a large tray with two mugs and a French press coffee carafe. "Every October, my family sails up the Connecticut River for some leaf-peeping. Do you think you might be boat-desensitized enough by then to go with us?"

Aaron opened his mouth, trying to focus on Cody's words, trying to respond when nothing made sense anymore.

Cody set his tray down with a clatter. "Aaron? What's wrong?"

"The job," he gasped, trying not to hyperventilate. "I didn't get it."

"Oh man, that's rough." Cody sat next to him and slung an arm around his shoulders. "You really liked that place."

"I didn't just *like* it. I was *counting* on it, which is so fucking *stupid* I can't even believe it." Heat swirled in his belly. "What *idiot* sells his house and quits his job before he has someplace else to go?"

"But you do have someplace else to go. Here."

"No, I don't. *You* have here. You have family. You have a home. You have a job—or you *could* have one if you bothered to take it."

Cody's eyes widened and he jerked back as if Aaron had struck him. "That's a little harsh, don't you think, Aaron?"

"You don't know what it's like." Aaron flung the blanket off his shoulders and lurched to his feet. "You wrap the Seaport, you wrap *Connecticut* around yourself like a freaking impenetrable cocoon. Hell, you live in the house you grew up in. You're so used to your support system that you don't even realize it's there."

"I know it's there. Believe me. I know how lucky I am."

"But you take it for granted because you *can*. You take risks, go on adventures, charge into the unknown, because you know they won't let you fall. You live life with no regrets." Aaron hunched his shoulders, bunching his fists. "I've got nothing *but* regrets."

"Do you regret what we did last night?" Cody's eyes were enormous in the early light, his voice soft. "Do you regret me?"

Aaron carded his hands through his hair, clutching it, the pain grounding him. "No. Of course not. But you're... you're...." He flung his arm out, gesturing at the Seaport, sleeping in the dawn light. "You're the Mystic man, letting song lyrics guide your life. I can't... I can't live with that kind of uncertainty."

"But, Aaron, nothing is ever certain. Nothing except change. Don't you think you owe it to yourself, to me, to *us*, to give this a chance?"

Aaron glanced around wildly. "It's too *different*. Christ, Cody, I can't even buy *potato chips* here. If I have to rebuild my life, at the very least I need familiar bricks."

"But you *hated* those bricks." Cody reached for him, but Aaron dodged, backing away until his hip grazed the starboard wheel. Cody clenched his fists, arms falling to his sides. "There's a difference between choosing something familiar because you love it and hiding behind it because you're terrified. That doesn't make you safe, Aaron. That makes you a prisoner. Don't you want to be free?"

"I tried it, all right? I tried to escape. I tried to convince someone that I could meld history and library science and make it meaningful for kids and they turned me down."

"That was one time, Aaron. *One*. Connecticut is lousy with prep schools. Don't you think your dreams deserve a second chance? Don't you think *we* deserve a chance?"

"But you won't *be* here." Cody flinched at Aaron's harsh tone. "You're leaving for a months-long backpacking trip.

Alone, for Chrissake. Who knows what will happen? I can't depend on you to be there for me."

"Aaron—"

"And I *shouldn't*, because you shouldn't have to bear that burden. You're the most wonderful man I've ever met, and I'll never forget you or the time we spent together. But I can't... I can't...." Aaron pressed his lips together, the despair welling in his chest threatening to burst out. "I have to get out of here. Pack up. Book a flight home."

"You don't have your car here. At least let me take you back to Clinton."

"No. I'll call an Uber." Because being in a car, so close to Cody, obviously scrambled Aaron's logic circuits. How else could Aaron explain last night's foolish certainty that he'd be able to make this leap—from coast to coast, career to career, man to man?

But it was a delusion, a fantasy of a perfect world, just like Mystic Seaport Village was the idealized version of something that had originally been far grittier and more dangerous. None of it was real. Reality was never this cheerful, this pleasant, this *perfect*. Reality was keeping your head down, maintaining a low profile, and dodging the fireballs life catapulted at your head.

Aaron climbed out of the boat and stood on the wharf, staring at Cody's beautiful, devastated face. "I'm sorry, Cody. You are amazing and I—" Aaron zipped up his jacket and shoved his hands in his pockets. "The leap was just too big for me." And he was still falling into the chasm.

He hurried through the deserted grounds of the Seaport as he ordered an Uber back to his Airbnb. He'd email HR.

Convince them to give him his job back. He'd come in early. Stay late. Prove to them that he was still the same Aaron.

Stick with what you know. At least you'll be safe. "Safe" had always been a fair trade-off for "happy," and it would be again.

It had to be.

The leaves on the trees outside Cody's living room window were just hitting their peak, and his first thought was *Aaron would love this.* But Aaron wouldn't see it because he was back in California, rooting through dusty archives, hiding from his own happiness. Heck, he probably never even saw the light of day.

Damn it. *Three weeks.* Aaron had been gone three weeks, and Cody still saw everything through an Aaron-centric lens. *Get over it, Cody. He's not coming back.*

He trudged down the stairs from his apartment as he pulled on his jacket. Since Eliza was still in the throes of morning-noon-and-night sickness, Cody walked Kaya to the bus stop every day, but this morning, Eliza was on the porch, helping Kaya into her backpack.

"Hey, Lize. Shouldn't you be resting?"

"I can't afford to put off any more projects." She hugged her sweater around herself, a little green around the gills. "Consequently, 'maintain' is my current mantra, which, in conjunction with a little reflexology and mainlining peppermints, is keeping me ambulatory. Barely."

Kaya tugged on his sleeve. "Uncle Cody, I've got another hey-you story to show my teacher today."

He grinned down at her, tweaking her shiny dark braid. "Yeah? Who's it about this time?"

"It's about you and Aaron."

He shared a dumbfounded glance with his sister, his stomach doing a barrel roll. She mouthed, *Sorry.* Cody shifted his gaze to Kaya's beaming face. "Is that so?"

"Yes. You and Aaron live upstairs, and we all go to Bishop's to pick apples and then on the boat to look at leaves, and when it snows we build a snow dragon in the backyard."

"That's...." He swallowed against the lump in his throat. "That's awesome, munchkin."

She glared at him. "Uncle *Cody.*"

"Right. No munchkins. Sorry. I forgot."

She grabbed his hand. "Come on. I want to show Jamie and Nica my story."

He let her drag him down the porch steps, and to his surprise, Eliza came with them. "Are you sure it's a good idea to venture so far from the porcelain?"

Eliza glowered at him, swallowing convulsively a couple of times. "Don't go there, Cody. I mean it. I want to talk to you before you leave for the Seaport."

"Okaaay." They neared the corner and Kaya raced off to join her friends, Cody and Eliza hanging back behind the cluster of other parents. "Why? Is something wrong?"

"Hiran said you're about to sign on to a long-term contract with him."

Cody sighed. "Yeah. At least three years as scrum master on this project."

"Don't do it."

Cody blinked. "Say what?"

"Don't. Do. It. Go on that stupid backpacking trip. Sail to Fiji. Go back to Alaska; I don't care."

"Wait a minute." He grabbed her elbow and pulled her back farther, under a maple with brilliant red leaves. "You *hated* the idea of the backpacking trip. And you've been trying to nail my feet under one of Hiran's desks for ages. Why the change in tune?"

She frowned, hugging her sweater tighter around her body, which was only just now showing the swell of the new baby. "Because you're not happy, Cody. You're... I don't know... *dimmer* than you've ever been in your life, and working for Hiran, much as I love the man, isn't going to fix that. You need one of your adventures to light you up again."

Cody plucked one of the leaves, smoothing it over his palm, and tracing its veins as he leaned against the tree trunk. "Thing is, Lize, the whole solo thing doesn't appeal to me so much anymore." In fact, it felt more like an obligation, the same old, same old.

Everyone he met on those trips was just like him—the trip was about *the trip*. They expected to be wowed because that's why they'd chosen the destination in the first place—like reading the end of a murder mystery before the beginning.

In his few days with Aaron, Cody had become addicted to *sharing*. If Cody had been able to take Aaron with him, his attitude would be completely different because the trip would be about *discovery*—the surprise and wonder of finding something new and loving it against all expectations.

I want that. And he couldn't have it, not unless he found someone else with Aaron's odd mixture of intelligence and naiveté. *But they still wouldn't be Aaron.*

The school bus rolled up, and the kids arranged themselves in a line like the six-year-old veterans they were, Kaya waving to them as she climbed aboard.

Eliza plucked the leaf out of Cody's hand and let it drift to the ground. "At the very least, keep your shifts at the Seaport."

"They're used to me being gone in the winter, and since I told them a month ago that I'd be leaving, I don't know if they've got a spot for me."

"You could *ask* them anyway, but do *something*, Cody, because seeing you this way is freaking me out." She put a hand on her belly. "And that can't be good for the baby."

Cody was surprised into a laugh. "Nicely played, Lize. I'll think about it, but I've got to run. There are three third-grade classes arriving at nine, and I'm on deck at the Sailing Center."

And the third-graders kept him busy and entertained— as did the fifth graders who showed up after lunch— enough to keep "The Boys of Summer" from constant mental replay anyway.

By the time the end of his shift rolled around at three, Cody had hit that point of combined exhaustion/euphoria that came from the satisfaction of a job well done. Maybe Eliza had a point—volunteering here fed his soul in a way that he'd miss if he was a full-time code monkey.

And since he'd promised his sister he'd scope things out, Cody headed over to the administrative offices. When he asked the volunteer services coordinator if they could use him over the winter, she looked at him as if he were mental.

"We can *always* use volunteers. Tell me when you're available, and I'll put you on the schedule."

He chuckled. "You make this too easy."

"Seriously, though, Cody, have you ever thought of applying for a regular staff position? You've got more seniority in actual hours spent here than half the staff anyway."

Cody blinked. "I... never thought of it. I'm a computer science major."

"You think we don't have an IT department? Think about it. In fact, talk to HR and see what they've got." She grimaced. "I'm going to hate myself for that. If you hire on as a regular employee, you'll leave a big gap in my roster."

"Don't make that leap quite yet. But I'll think about it."

In truth, Cody needed something to break the link between the Seaport and Aaron that still existed in his mind, as if he'd run aground on a mental sandbar, unable to move on. Maybe this was the way to do it—alter his relationship with the Seaport, forget Aaron, and make his sister happy at the same time.

What the heck. Since he was here, he might as well test the waters. He reversed course, strolling over to Lewis House near the South Gate where HR was located. He held the door open for a couple of women, but when he entered himself, he nearly ran into a guy in a suit on his way out.

"Oops. Sorry, I—"

"Cody?"

The sound of that voice, the one that had haunted his dreams, made Cody stumble and ram his shoulder into the doorframe. "Aaron? What are you doing here?"

Aaron—and it was him, Cody wasn't just hallucinating—smoothed the hair at his nape. "Well... I... ah... I'm filling out my new hire paperwork."

Cody's heart beat loud in his ears. "You what?"

Aaron smiled tentatively. "I'm officially on the staff at Mystic Seaport Museum. Librarian and archivist. So I guess I'm a Mystic man too."

"How... how long have you been back in Connecticut?"

"A couple of weeks."

"How can you have been back for a couple of weeks? You've only been *gone* for three."

"Well, ten days, but you know." He shrugged one shoulder. "Rounding."

"Aaron." Cody's growl must have startled Aaron as much as it did Cody because he tugged at his tie as if it were choking him.

"I was kind of hoping you'd be glad to see me."

"Ten days, Aaron. Ten whole *days* and you didn't bother to come see me? Call me? Hell, send a freaking *text?*"

"I didn't want a repeat of what happened last time."

Cody stilled, although his breath still came in rapid puffs. What did that mean? Aaron didn't want to see him? Didn't want them to be together? "A repeat of what exactly?"

Aaron paled. "God, Cody, your face." He glanced over his shoulder. "Let's go outside, okay? Where we can talk privately?"

"Privately. In the middle of the Seaport. With visitors all over the freaking path."

"There's safety in numbers?"

"Well, you'd know all about *safety*." Cody couldn't keep the edge out of his voice, because damn it, it *hurt*.

Aaron winced. "I deserved that. But please. Hear me out?"

"Fine." Cody spun around and stalked through the door. He strode into the middle of the sidewalk and turned to face Aaron. "Here we are. Outside."

Aaron huffed a laugh, taking Cody's elbow and drawing him out of the middle of traffic. "Look. I didn't want a repeat of my meltdown, okay? *That's* what I meant."

Cody crossed his arms, still not ready to give in. "I thought you went back to California."

"I did. Long enough to sign the papers on my condo sale, pack up my life, and put everything in storage."

"But you said—"

"That I was planning to get my old job back?" Cody nodded. "Yeah, that was the plan for maybe half the flight back to LA. But then I remembered a couple of things."

"Like what?"

"Fresh lobster. The sunrise over the water, as seen from your boat." He took a step closer. "And your face when I told you I was leaving."

Cody winced. "I probably looked like a beached cod."

"You looked exactly like I felt every time my parents pulled another runner. Betrayed." Aaron traced Cody's cheek with the tip of one finger. "I... I have something to say to you. If you can forgive me at least enough to listen for a couple of minutes."

Cody made a point of obviously checking his watch. "Okay. I guess I can spare you that much."

Aaron took a deep breath. "Julia Morgan. Maria Tallchief. Katherine Goble Johnson." His expression was expectant, hopeful.

But Cody was clueless. "Huh?"

"Remember, you asked me for three stories from history that ended well. Julia Morgan was the first licensed female architect in California. Among other things, she designed a little shack called Hearst Castle. Maria Tallchief was the first prima ballerina for the New York City Ballet, and the first Native American granted the title. Mrs. Johnson—"

"I remember now. WOC and NASA mathematician who helped put John Glenn in orbit."

Aaron nodded. "I know that's not exactly *regaling*, but that can happen later. I picked stories about women because—"

"Because Kaya said history needed more girls in it." Cody's heart floated free in his chest, bumping around his rib cage, until Aaron's tentative smile sent it soaring.

"I don't belong *in* a place—I belong *with* a person. For me, that person is you."

"Okay, how am I supposed to stay mad at you when you say things like that?"

Aaron reached out and hooked their forefingers together. "I hope you won't stay mad at me at all. We've known each other such a short time. I know what *I* hope for the future, but I didn't want—I still don't want to turn into a… an albatross around your neck. I needed to get my ducks in a row before I called you so you wouldn't be, I don't know. Responsible for my happiness, I guess."

"Have you ever *looked* at ducks, Aaron? They're *always* in a row." He snatched his hand away, but Aaron caught his finger again and Cody didn't fight it. "And suppose I *want* to be responsible for making you happy?"

"That's a very different thing, and it needs to go both ways." He drew Cody closer. "I've got a job now, a place to live. I even had a drive-away service bring my car cross-country, so I can meet you on equal footing." His lips quirked in a lopsided smile. "So what do you say to some reciprocal responsibility?"

Cody curled his finger, linking it more securely with Aaron's. "I have one demand. It's non-negotiable."

Aaron's swallowed, his Adam's apple sliding enticingly above the collar of his white dress shirt. "I'd say 'anything,' but you know I've got my limits. I'm working on them, but—"

"No more putting our happiness on hold for organizationally challenged waterfowl. I don't care if your freaking ducks are scattered from hell to breakfast, I'm not waiting for them to line up. Our future starts now. Tonight. Come home with me. We can have dinner with the family, and you can regale Kaya with stories of Julia Morgan, Maria Tallchief and… and…."

"Katherine Goble Johnson."

"Exactly. Then afterward—" Cody glanced around to make sure nobody was close enough to overhear. He leaned forward to murmur in Aaron's ear. "*Afterward, I can revel in your skin again.*"

Aaron shivered visibly. "I… I'd like that."

"She wrote another story, by the way. Kaya."

"She did? Does Amelia Earhart sail up the Connecticut River on a leaf-peeping adventure?"

"Not quite. The river and leaves make an appearance, as does Bishop's Orchard again, but there's no Amelia

Earhart in sight." He rested his hand on Aaron's chest, and Aaron's heartbeat was as erratic as his own. "It's about you and me."

Aaron's eyebrows traveled up his forehead. "Us?"

"Yep. So if you don't want to destroy her faith in history forever...."

Aaron covered Cody's hand with his own. "We'll have to make this story end happily ever after."

Aaron's kiss, soft, warm, but totally safe for work, promised exactly that.

CHAPTER
TEN

A year later.

"Hey, Aaron." Cody's voice, cheerful and dear, carried easily on the bright hillside, even though he was on the other side of the next row of apple trees. "I've got the perfect idea for our trip."

Aaron peered out between the leaves of his own target tree to see Cody grinning at him. *Who needs the sun when I've got him?* "Our trip?"

"You and me." He wandered toward Aaron, one hand swinging an empty bucket, the other swooping through the air. "Sailing."

"On the water?"

"That's usually how it's done."

Aaron placed a pair of apples in the bucket at his feet and ducked out from under the tree to fix Cody with a mock glare. "You know, when you said you wanted to set sail on our new life, I thought you were speaking *metaphorically*."

"You're a Mystic man now, Aaron. Ships and boats are unavoidable. Besides, you did fine on the river cruises."

"Yes, but that was a few hours on perfectly calm days with land in sight on both sides the whole time."

"It's a progression. I think your fear has more to do with lack of experience than actual, you know, *fear*. After another summer of sailing lessons, you'll be ready for the Sound. Maybe even Cape Cod."

"Don't press your luck," Aaron growled, but couldn't be too intimidating in the face of Cody's infectious grin.

"I wouldn't be true to my job as a sailing instructor if I didn't at least try. Then once you're acclimated...." He waggled his eyebrows. "We can have some *real* fun."

Aaron shook his head as he reached for his half-full bucket. "Your idea of fun—"

"Oh, come on, Aaron. Aruba? Jamaica?"

Aaron paused, narrowing his eyes as he studied Cody's mischievous expression. "You've been listening to your dad's music again, haven't you? The Beach Boys?"

Cody's grinned, obviously unrepentant. "Guilty." He linked his arm with Aaron's as they strolled toward where the rest of the family was still picking fruit. "But the day we met, you said it yourself. Traveling is for sharing experiences with the people you love. That's what 'Kokomo' is about, right?"

"Maybe. Okay, yes. It is. But that doesn't mean you're getting me on a boat."

"You've been on a boat with me before, if you recall." Cody leaned closer, murmuring in Aaron's ear. "Good things happen when we're on boats together."

Heat rushed up Aaron's throat when he remembered some of those good things. "Can't argue with that," he muttered. "But—"

"Hey." Cody caught Aaron's hand, pulling him into the shade between two trees. "We won't do anything that makes you uncomfortable. We can stay docked at the Seaport for our entire vacation if you want. But think about it." Cody kissed him, his lips soft and warm from the sun. "Okay?"

Aaron smiled down at him—because how could he not? —and stroked Cody's shaggy hair back from his forehead. "Okay."

"That's all I ask, you know," Cody murmured, expression turning serious. "You don't have to go along with *all* my harebrained schemes."

"I know. But as you said, good things happen when I do, so every scheme at least deserves consideration." Aaron shaded his eyes, peering up at the sun. "You know, I thought Kaya was exaggerating when she drew those giant suns in her pictures of the family at Bishop's." He shot Cody a wry smile. "Especially now that I've been in Connecticut long enough to know autumn weather can be extremely unpredictable. But she got it right."

"Yeah." Cody leaned into his shoulder. "It's weird. We always come out here to pick apples around the second week of October, and in my memory, it's always been a perfect day, just like this."

The sun had nothing on the warmth in Aaron's chest. Because in the months since he'd moved to Connecticut, even in February which (as Cody had once told him) totally sucked, all the days had been perfect to him because he'd spent part of each one—and most of his nights—with Cody.

Then, when the lease on his apartment was up last month, they'd moved in together, into Eliza and Hiran's newly renovated carriage house.

A home. A job he loved. A boyfriend he loved even more. A year ago, Aaron would never have believed it was possible.

Kaya raced up to them, seemingly all knees and elbows after her latest growth spurt. She held up her own bucket. "Is this enough, Uncle Cody?"

Cody tweaked her braid. "You think a dozen apples is enough to keep you in sauce, pie, and cider all winter?"

"If it was just me." She glowered at her baby brother, currently trying to shove his entire fist into his mouth while strapped in a baby carrier on Hiran's chest. "But that Shaan eats a *lot* of applesauce."

"Well, then. Back at it." Cody chuckled as she stalked down the hill with another glare at her brother, spoiling the effect when she patted him on his round tummy, and Aaron was hit by a sneaker wave of tenderness.

He set down his apple bucket and cuddled up against Cody's back, nuzzling his nape.

"Mmmmm." Cody leaned back into his embrace. "Not that I'm complaining, but what was that for?"

"Nothing. Just that I love you."

Cody twisted around to face Aaron, letting his empty bucket drop to the ground. "That's not nothing, babe. That's *everything*. And I love you too." He lifted his chin for another kiss, which they kept PG since *all* of Cody's family—not just Eliza's crew, but his parents, his brother, George, aunts, uncles, and cousins whom Aaron had stopped trying to count—were running around the orchard, and they never knew when one of them would pop out from behind a tree.

Cody wrapped his arms around Aaron's waist and squeezed, hitting exactly the wrong place. Wincing, Aaron sucked in a breath.

Immediately, Cody let go, stepping back. "What's wrong? Did I hurt you?"

"No. That is, sort of, but it's not your fault." Aaron dropped his gaze, scratching the back of his head. "See, there's this thing...."

"You know, for a librarian, you suck at words sometimes."

Aaron sighed. "I know. But admitting to impulsiveness has never worked out well for me."

Cody's grin bloomed. "Impulsive, Aaron? You? Tell me."

"I got a... a tattoo."

"Really? Another one?"

"No. I just finished the first one." Aaron raised his T-shirt to display the new ink in the center of his bookplate tattoo: Cody's name in a rustic font, entwined with an anchor. "Since I'm out of circulation and berthed here for good...."

"*Oh.*" He stroked Aaron's skin with a feather touch, his smile incandescent.

"You're my safe harbor, sweetheart. Now and always."

Cody threaded his hands through Aaron's hair. "And you're my anchor, because wherever you are, that's where I'll be." He drew Aaron's head down for a lingering kiss. "Now, about that sailing trip...."

Author's Note

I lived in Connecticut for three years while attending graduate school. During that time, I met my Curmudgeonly Husband, who's Connecticut born and raised—although interestingly enough, I met him in Vermont and our first six months living together were spent in Washington, DC.

Like Cody does for Aaron, CH introduced me to things about Connecticut that he knew and loved: Killam's Point, The Place, Bishop's Orchards, and of course Mystic Seaport. The story Cody tells about drifting out to sea with his cousin Kenny actually happened to CH and *his* cousin Kenny (and I may have had a reaction similar to Aaron's).

One day, on a hike in the hills above New Haven (during which I had a panic attack of my own while standing on a steep slope—I am not a fan of heights), we met a family with a young son. He took one look at Hartford in the distance and asked, "How come it doesn't take us an hour to *see* Hartford?"

It's still one of the best questions I've ever heard.

a message from

ej

Dear Reader,

Thank you so much for reading *Mystic Man*, my homage to Curmudgeonly Husband's home state. I loved revisiting Connecticut (at least virtually), and I hope you enjoyed the trip as well! I'd be immensely grateful if you'd take a moment to leave a review at the retailer and any other site you use for reviews. Believe me, reviews make an *enormous* difference to the health and well-being of books (and not incidentally, to their associated authors!).

Wondering what to read next? If you're a fan of contemporary romance, you might like *Clickbait*, where love blossoms at a construction site, between a prickly web designer and a family-focused electrician. If you're in the mood for something a little less, er, reality-based, there's my Mythmatched story universe—paranormal romantic comedy, beginning with *Cutie and the Beast*, where a cursed fae warrior turned psychologist clashes with his determined temporary office manager. As you might expect, hi-jinks ensue!

Pop on over to my website, https://ejrussell.com, for all the deets on my books—my paranormal rom-coms and mysteries, my contemporary romances, and my one lone historical. If you're an audio fan, you can find the audio scoop there too. *Mystic Man*, for instance, is narrated by the wonderful Kirt Graves. (The QR code below will get you there with your smartphone camera or other code reader.)

Would you like exclusive content and ARC giveaways, not to mention gratuitous dance videos? Then I'd love for you to join me in E.J. Russell's Reality Optional, my Facebook fan group (https://facebook.com/groups/reality.optional). My newsletter is the place to get the latest dish on new releases, sales, and more. I promise I only send one out when I've got...well...news. You can subscribe here: https://ejrussell.com/newsletter.

All my best,
—E

Also by
ej

Paranormal Romance
Mythmatched Universe
Fae Out of Water Trilogy
Cutie and the Beast
The Druid Next Door
Bad Boy's Bard

Supernatural Selection Trilogy
Single White Incubus
Vampire With Benefits
Demon on the Down-Low

Other Mythmatched Romances
Howling on Hold
Possession in Session
Witch Under Wraps
Cursed is the Worst
The Skinny on Djinni
Assassin by Accident (part of Carnival of Mysteries)

Quest Investigations Mysteries
Five Dead Herrings
The Hound of the Burgervilles
The Lady Under the Lake
Death on Denial

At Odds with the Gods (A Mythmatched/Purgatory Playhouse crossover)

Mythmatchedlets (Mythmatched companion stories, free to newsletter subscribers in ebook form, collected in one paperback volume: *Second First Date, Rusty's Really Bad Day, First Flight, Getting the Band Together, Purgatory Postscript, A Very Quest Solstice*)

Magic Emporium Series (shared world)
Purgatory Playhouse

Enchanted Occasions Series
Best Beast
Nudging Fate
Devouring Flame

Ghost Townies Series
Ghostridden

Legend Tripping Series
Stumptown Spirits
Wolf's Clothing

Art Medium Series
The Artist's Touch
Tested in Fire
Art Medium: The Complete Collection (omnibus edition)

Royal Powers Series (shared world)
Duking It Out

Duke the Hall
King's Ex

Science Fiction
Sun, Moon, and Stars Series
Partnership
Principles

Interdimensional Time Bureau
Monster Till Midnight

Historical Romance
Silent Sin

Contemporary Romance
Camera Shy
Summer Kitchen
The Thomas Flair
Mystic Man
For a Good Time, Call... (A Bluewater Bay novel, with
Anne Tenino)

Christmas Kisses (holiday shorts)
The Probability of Mistletoe
An Everyday Hero
A Swants Soiree

Geeklandia Series
The Boyfriend Algorithm (M/F)
Clickbait

Writing as Nelle Heran

(traditional cozy mystery)

Crafty Sleuth Series (with C.K. Eastland)
Die Cut
Mixed Media
Found Objects (*coming soon*)

About the
Author

E.J. Russell (she/her), author of the award-winning Mythmatched paranormal romance series, writes LGBTQ+ romance and mystery in a rainbow of flavors. Count on high snark, low angst, and happy endings.

Reality? Eh, not so much.

She's married to Curmudgeonly Husband, a man who cares even less about sports than she does. Luckily, C.H. also loves to cook, or all three of their children (Lovely Daughter and Darling Sons A and B) would have survived on nothing but Cheerios, beef jerky, and Satsuma mandarins (the extent of E.J.'s culinary skill set).

E.J. also writes traditional cozy mystery as Nelle Heran. She lives in rural Oregon, enjoys visits from her wonderful adult children, and indulges in good books, red wine, and the occasional hyperbole.

News & Social Media:
Website: https://ejrussell.com
Newsletter: https://ejrussell.com/newsletter

Acknowledgements

As ever, a heartfelt thank you to my readers for following me as I sail from genre to genre. I'm so grateful that you're keeping me company on this journey!

Thanks to Tricia Kristufek and her team for editing, to L.C. Chase for the cover that perfectly captures Cody, and of course, to my family—Jim, Hana, Nick, Ross, and Billy —for anchoring me so well.